GUNFIRE
MOUNTAIN

Center Point
Large Print

Also by Ed La Vanway and available from
Center Point Large Print:

Caprock Range
Outlaw Valley

**This Large Print Book carries the
Seal of Approval of N.A.V.H.**

GUNFIRE MOUNTAIN

Ed La Vanway

CENTER POINT LARGE PRINT
THORNDIKE, MAINE

This Center Point Large Print edition
is published in the year 2019 by arrangement with
Golden West Literary Agency.

First US edition: Avalon Books

The text of this Large Print edition is unabridged.
In other aspects, this book may vary
from the original edition.
Printed in the United States of America
on permanent paper.
Set in 16-point Times New Roman type.

ISBN: 978-1-64358-068-5 (hardcover)
ISBN: 978-1-64358-072-2 (paperback)

Library of Congress Cataloging-in-Publication Data

Names: La Vanway, Ed, author.
Title: Gunfire mountain / Ed La Vanway.
Description: Center Point Large Print edition. | Thorndike, Maine :
    Center Point Large Print, 2019.
Identifiers: LCCN 2018047173| ISBN 9781643580685
    (hardcover : alk. paper) | ISBN 9781643580722
    (paperback : alk. paper)
Subjects: LCSH: Western stories. | Large type books.
Classification: LCC PS3562.A126 G86 2019 | DDC 813/.54—dc23
LC record available at https://lccn.loc.gov/2018047173

GUNFIRE
MOUNTAIN

CHAPTER I

It was early morning with a high-sailing moon sifting its beams through the sycamores to make the rushing waters of Little Goose Creek seem strewn with bits of polished silver. From mid-channel the three riders surged out of the stream on the far bank, and climbed the slope to level ground. In the gloom of bosque, Sheriff Oscar Rodin brought his sorrel to a halt. He dismounted.

Deputy Wade Smollet stopped his horse, too, but kept to his saddle.

Johnny McVay, the sheriff's nephew from Wyoming, did the same.

Sheriff Rodin, a gaunt man with well-trimmed sandy mustaches and chin whiskers, snapped a lucifer aflame and hunkered down. He stood erect and moved to another spot and knelt again. Before the match guttered out, he had examined the roadbed thoroughly. Besides the ruts left in the moist earth by the wheels of the southbound stagecoach, whose destination of Grief Hill was in the opposite direction, the sheriff found more recent hoofprints headed away from the town.

Tall in mottled moonlight and shadow, Sheriff Rodin moved closer to his deputy. Smollet had on an uncreased black hat. He was a chunky man with a round face and a long hooked nose.

"Two horses," Sheriff Rodin said to him. "They came this way, just like I knowed they would."

"You figure they stopped at Sammy Lee Dilts's place?"

"Where else would they stop?"

The deputy was silent.

"You see, Wade, they don't know yet they've been identified."

"Luther Blaine knew. The other man didn't. Oscar, are you trying to tell me that kid, Sammy Lee, has guts enough to help pull a robbing and killing?"

Rodin said, "Why else would he have been riding around with Luther Blaine? And Sammy Lee's got a mean look in his eye, Wade. Born with it."

"Too bad Barlow didn't see both of them."

The sheriff said, "Uh-huh." Gathering up the bridle reins, he turned out a stirrup and went into the saddle. Somewhat grouchily, he said, "Well, come on, boys."

Bit chains jingling, saddle leather creaking, horses' hoofs almost soundless on the springy humus, the three of them continued on. Following the road, they emerged onto a broad prairie where the trail forked. One trail went straight ahead to the far-off moonlit mountain. Sheriff Rodin reined in at the fork.

"Beat it on out to the Fiddleback, Wade, and tell Miss Connie about her pa. Tell her I'm all broke up about it. Tell her I'm on the trail of the killers and I won't rest a minute till I get them." The sheriff paused. "I've been pretty strict with them Fiddleback fellers."

"You sure have, Oscar," the deputy said. "Well, I'll be getting along." He touched his horse with a spur, lifting him to a trot and then to a canter.

The sheriff said to his nephew, "Wade's a good feller."

"Yeah," Johnny said. "I saw Barlow Clesson's body, but I never did understand just what happened."

"I guess you didn't. I liked to never got you awake. Barlow won a potful of money in a poker game last night. When he headed for home, he was robbed. Blaine took him off in the brush and knifed him. Barlow wasn't quite dead. He crawled back into the road and stopped the stage."

"And he didn't recognize but one of them?"

"You heard Wade, didn't you?"

"Why, sure." In daylight, Johnny McVay appeared slim and yellow-haired. He wore his broad-brimmed Stetson telescoped on top and had a blue silk neckerchief knotted above his calico shirt. His vest was maroon corduroy. His pants were dark wool, and tucked into high-heeled boots. His spurs had large blunt rowels with small iron clogs and chains that sometimes jingled. The flap had been cut off the holster which held his Remington .44, and a .44 carbine rested in the boot under his left leg. "That old rawhider, Barlow, was filthy rich. Imagine him letting somebody kill him over gambling money."

Sheriff Rodin said, "Well, let's be riding," and Johnny McVay reined his blazed-face black gelding over beside his uncle's sorrel.

They followed the north fork, the moonlight silhouetting not only the mountain range to the west but also to the north, showing them the timber of Big Goose Creek, into which this stream debouched. Big Goose Creek then cut through rolling hills and flowed toward Red River.

"We didn't have any breakfast. Not even coffee. What was the rush, Uncle Oscar? You're not hurrying now."

"I plumb forgot about it."

"Wade's making a mighty long ride on an empty stomach. The hotel dining room was open for business, serving the stage passengers. While you were rousting me out, why didn't you let Wade eat?"

"Pablo don't work nights, and somebody had to saddle your horse."

Johnny McVay said, "That's not a very good way of doing things."

"Wade had some cold coffee at home. I heard Lucy tell him where the meat and biscuits was. If he didn't grab a bite to eat, it was his own fault."

"But I heard him say, 'Boy, that ham smells good. Ham and eggs.'"

"Johnny, if you don't like the way I'm running my office, why don't you go on back to Wyoming? I didn't send for you. A body would think you was the sheriff, instead of me."

"I'm not trying to tell you how to run your office, Uncle Oscar."

"Sounds like it. And you ain't as growed-up as you think you are."

"I've grown quite a bit since you saw me."

"Fifteen years? I reckon you have."

Johnny said, "I wouldn't have come down here if you had kept writing. After you wrote that bragging letter about being elected sheriff, and then not another line, ma started to worry about you."

"Well, she ain't worrying now, is she? Didn't you write to her?"

"I sent her a telegram."

They rode on in silence. Finally Sheriff Rodin said, "Yeah, Johnny, I plumb forgot about eating. But I've been so rough on Barlow Clesson's Fiddleback fellers. And with the shoe on the other foot now, so to speak. Everybody excited about a couple of killers being loose. I didn't want to be seen sitting there calmly guzzling coffee."

"So you and Wade and I hightailed it out of town just for appearances."

"I reckon so," the sheriff admitted. He stopped

his horse. "We're getting right close to Sammy Lee Dilts's place and we can't do nothing till daylight. Let's ride into the woods and wait a spell."

Back in the gloom of the timber, Sheriff Rodin dismounted to wrap a bridle rein around a low limb.

Johnny McVay only ground-hitched the split reins of his gelding. "How much poker winnings did they take off of Barlow Clesson?" he asked.

"Barlow Clesson had nine thousand dollars on him, all told. You know, Johnny, that just goes to show you what whisky will do. If Barlow had been sober, he would still be alive. The Fiddleback keeps rooms rented permanent at the hotel, and that's where Barlow would have gone."

It began getting light overhead, and birds started chirping on their tree-limb roosts. Sheriff Rodin was looking north. "Ain't no watchdog down there to worry about. Sammy Lee did have one, about as close to him as a brother. He started courting Rebecca Casper, though, and danged if that dog didn't take up with her. It won't pay no mind to Sammy Lee at all, now."

Suddenly the sheriff's expression became intent. He sniffed the air, nostrils flaring. He glanced at his nephew.

"You ain't got no cigareet lit, have you, Johnny?"

"No."

"I smell tobacco smoke. Sammy Lee don't smoke. Then Luther Blaine is sure enough there."

"You're fairly certain, then, that Blaine and Dilts are the men you want?"

"Dead or alive." Sheriff Rodin kept sniffing. "On a dampish morning like this, I can smell smells a mile or more. Just now I got a whiff of bacon and coffee.

"No fooling, Johnny." Sheriff Rodin glanced up through the tree crowns at the brightening sky.

Johnny loosened his Remington in the holster. "It's daylight. Let's get it over with."

"Hold on now. Not so fast. Hear that cow?"

"She needs to be milked," Johnny said.

"That's what I mean. When she quits bawling, Sammy Lee will be squeezing her tits. Blaine will be in bed. Sammy Lee ain't no hand with a six-shooter, but he can sure knock the frost off a punkin with a rifle. And if he's butting that cow in the flank, he won't get his hands on a rifle."

The cow mooed regularly, but Rodin said, "By the time I mosey on down there, Sammy Lee will be doing his chores." The sheriff drew his six-shooter and gave it a careful inspection. "Stay right here, now, Johnny, till you hear me holler."

Johnny said, "But they're guilty of a murder already. Those men won't surrender, Uncle Oscar."

13

"I'll go in and get Blaine and handcuff him, and when Sammy Lee brings his milk in, I'll nab him."

"Sounds easy. You sure wouldn't do that up in Wyoming."

"Oh, I don't know. I've been a Ranger and a U. S. marshal. City marshal twice. Nobody hereabouts has criticized me except the Fiddleback."

Johnny offered no comment, and Sheriff Rodin moved off through the brush.

Johnny McVay thought he could wait it out. Suddenly he realized he couldn't, and he knew then why his ma had worried. Oscar Rodin didn't have sense enough to be afraid. Turning to his saddle, Johnny drew his Sunday gun, his sixteen-shot Henry rifle. He slowly jacked a cartridge into the firing chamber, keeping the sound to a minimum. Afterwards he lowered the hammer of the self-cocking rifle, which you were supposed to load on Sunday and shoot all week. He contemplated removing his noisy spurs, but he didn't. He, too, went on afoot, walking much faster than his uncle, making slight commotion as he picked his way through the underbrush.

Johnny angled away from the trail his uncle had taken and went down the head-high creek bank to the first bottom, hurrying along at the edge of the water. Little Goose Creek rushed down a narrow, boulder-choked channel, then broadened into an expanse of slow-flowing water which eddied through a corner of a pole-fenced corral.

Briefly, Johnny stopped to listen.

A crow was cawing loudly enough to be heard above the rapids upstream, and one passed directly overhead, wings beating rhythmically. Otherwise there was silence, except for, now and then, the cow.

The shake roofs of outbuildings were visible, but Sammy Lee Dilts's house, a double cabin joined by a breezeway, couldn't be seen.

Hurrying on, Johnny came to a jackstraw pile of driftwood logs that Dilts had collected for firewood. Here at the edge of the stream stood a big black cast-iron kettle, used for boiling clothes on washdays and for rendering lard at hog-killing time. Near the pile of logs was a sawbuck. A double-bitted ax was sticking in the splitting block close by, and a path led up the bank and alongside the corral fence.

Again Johnny stopped to listen.

Because of the creek bank, he couldn't see much, but he was close. Overhead a smudge of woodsmoke showed above the place where Dilts's house sat, and off to the north and east were more breakfast-fire columns. Bundles of fleecy clouds wafted about and as Johnny glanced up, the wispy edge of one was slowly flicking out, searching the blue.

Johnny had no way of telling how close to

the house his uncle was. Suddenly then it came to him that the cow had stopped mooing. It was time to go.

Carbine in both hands, Johnny ascended the path, gradually getting a view of the nester layout. Now he could see the well and the back porch.

He felt sure that Sammy Lee was in the barnlot, but he had reached a front corner of the corral before he espied Sammy Lee and the cow on the north side of the crib.

Sammy Lee generally wore a store suit, but now he had on a brush-jumper and bib overalls. He was big-boned, bare-headed and light-complexioned. At this moment, Sammy Lee stood erect with a bucket of milk. Moving closer to the crib, he untied a rope, and a calf came bounding forward.

Sammy Lee Dilts saw Johnny McVay then. Features twisting, he shouted, "Watch out, Luke!" Dropping the bucket, he ran, ducking into the wagonway of the barn.

Johnny McVay drew and fired, mostly to remind Sammy Lee to stay there unless he came out with his hands up.

Where was the sheriff?

Johnny heard a clatter inside the house, but the man who appeared on the porch wasn't Rodin. He was a squat, thick-shouldered, bearded hombre, blazing away with a gun. Johnny shot

16

and he pitched off the porch. There was another man shooting, too, white powdersmoke fogging around him there in the hall. Johnny dropped him and watched him try to crawl away. He soon lay still. Then there had been three of them. Someone had misfigured.

Sheriff Rodin trotted out of the brush south of the house. "Why didn't you shoot Sammy Lee?"

"I couldn't. He wasn't armed."

"Why, this ain't no game we're playing. It's law work. You ought to of shot him in the leg. Now he's gone—jumped the fence and hightailed it."

Johnny said, "He can't possibly get away. I'll cut his sign and catch him for you."

Disgusted, Rodin shook his head. "No good will of come of it." Approaching with drawn sixgun, the sheriff leveled a forefinger. "Why tote that Henry? You don't use it."

"I never leave it on my saddle. It's a gift from Wells Fargo, and I don't want anyone to steal it."

Rodin was standing over the bearded man. "Luther, did you help rob and kill Barlow Clesson?"

"Yes."

Lifting his gaze, the sheriff noticed the man in the hallway. Startled, he took a step backward. "Why, that's Joe Hooker. Joe, why in the name of heaven did you do that? All the ranches in this valley ain't worth a man's life."

17

When Joe Hooker didn't answer, Rodin's chin-whiskered face contorted.

The man lying near Rodin's boots said, "Don't accuse Joe of it, Oscar. He didn't even know about it. Been too drunk to know anything."

Sheriff Rodin paled. Not guilty—nevertheless Joe Hooker was shot to doll rags. "Who was your pardner, Luther, Sammy Lee?"

Rodin got no reply. Slowly he removed his hat. Luther Blaine was dead.

Walking over beside his uncle, Johnny McVay reached for the pistol Blaine had dropped. Rodin himself went onto the porch and into the hallway, hat in hand.

Joe Hooker was a bandy-legged small man, gray and wrinkled. His rheumy eyes were pain-racked. The bullet having gone clean through him, his vest and shirt were bloody both front and rear. Rodin holstered his gun and put on his hat. When Johnny came into the hallway, the sheriff squared around.

"Well, you smart-alec kid, see what you've done? Killed an innocent man. Why didn't you wait and let me do like I said?"

"I wasn't thinking about your tin badge when I shot him. I was wondering if I could get him before he could get me." Hunkering down in order to read Hooker's eyes, Johnny asked, "Why did you shoot at me, old man?"

"Figured you was a Fiddlebacker."

"Them fancy duds of yours are what done it," the sheriff said. "Joe's carried on a feud with the Fiddleback for twenty-five years. Barlow Clesson's dead, Joe. Robbed and killed. That's why we're here."

"I ain't sorry about him. Or myself, either."

"If you didn't know anything about it, you can't tell us where the money is, can you?"

"No."

Johnny McVay stood erect, to have his uncle jab him in the ribs.

"I smell bread a-burning."

Johnny McVay jingled his spurs into the kitchen. Standing the carbine near the cupboard, he grabbed up a dishcloth, lowered the oven door and dragged the pan of biscuits out, charred around the edges. After that he pushed the coffeepot to a cooler spot on the stove, diminishing its spout of steam.

Two places had been laid at the table. In the center stood a whisky bottle, three-quarters full, with a half-dozen empties in a row near the woodbox.

Johnny McVay took a small drink.

It appeared that Blaine and Hooker, waiting for the biscuits to get done, had sat at the table guzzling liquor until Sammy Lee's yell had brought them away. There was an over-turned chair and another was shoved far back.

Johnny returned to the hallway and stood

19

there with his uncle, looking down at Hooker.

Sheriff Rodin appeared helpless. "I ain't much of a hand with gunshot wounds. See if you can find some clean cloth and medicine."

Johnny said, "Use bedsheets and whisky." Johnny brought the bottle from the kitchen. He uncorked it and took a long pull.

"How long have you been drinking, Johnny?"

"Oh, I started drinking when I became free, white and twenty-one, Uncle Oscar."

Sheriff Rodin glared. Turning away, he entered the room across from the kitchen and emerged with a blanket and a sheet. He handed the blanket to Johnny.

"Go spread that over Blaine."

Johnny went down into the yard, covered Blaine, and stood there looking around carefully, not wanting to stop a bullet from a hidden marksman, such as Sammy Lee Dilts. Johnny was conscious of the rail-fenced hogpen north of the barnlot, and his ears were aware of the still-frightened chickens. The horses, too, had forgotten; three of them had their ears tipped toward the house. There was no one around.

Coming out on the porch, Sheriff Rodin turned toward the tin washbasin beside the brassbound cedar bucket. Filling the basin, Rodin said, "Come and help me get a bandage on Joe, Johnny."

Working gently, they got Joe Hooker's upper body bare and the holes disinfected and bound.

Dilts's shirts were too large for the oldster, but they put one on him, anyhow.

Rodin said, "Think you'll live, Joe?"

"If I don't, who'll give a dang?"

"Your daughter."

"And me," Johnny said.

"I don't blame you, kid. Not a bit. I come out and asked for it."

Rodin knelt down. "Get hold of him, Johnny, and let's take him in yonder, put him to bed." When they had Hooker as comfortable as he could be under the circumstances, Rodin asked, "Where's your clothes and stuff, Joe?"

"At Saul Delbert's."

"Want us to take you there? It's a mite far for Doc Mueller."

"Take me to town."

"Can you make it?"

Irritably Hooker said, "Leave me alone, can't you?"

Sheriff Rodin stepped out of the room, motioning for Johnny. "Let's see about that grub."

"Let's see about our horses."

"Well, you want me to go?"

"No. You eat. I'll just take another taste of that liquor," Johnny said, and when he had done so, he left.

CHAPTER II

The stovepipes beyond the cornfields and dead snags were no longer plumed with smoke, Johnny noticed, glancing north. West, he saw sunlight on the mountain; even the canyons were visible. To the southwest, scattered cattle grazed peaceably on open range, while atop one lone tree far out on the prairie a crow bobbed and cawed raucously. Nearby, a field lark, yellow breast brilliant, rose straight off the grass, warbling, and the bosque seemed to be working alive with racketing jays.

Johnny found the sorrel easily but he didn't find the sheriff's saddle gun, nor his own blazed-face black gelding. The ground-tied horse hadn't strayed. It had been stolen. Sammy Lee, of course. Angered, Johnny stepped astraddle the sorrel.

A brown-and-white mongrel with silky ears was squatted on its haunches in the front yard. It emitted a series of barks when the sorrel shook the brush, but the dog didn't move. When Johnny McVay rode into the sunlit clearing, it still didn't move. It only yawned widely, tongue curling, and thumped dust with its tail.

Johnny said, "What's your name, dog?"

"Spot," the girl said.

Sandy head uncovered, Sheriff Rodin stood on

the porch, and the girl bestrode a barebacked roan mare. About seventeen, she had curly chestnut hair with a pretty face that was strained with doubt and fear and worry.

There was a warning for silence in Rodin's chin-whiskered face. "Where's your horse, Johnny?"

"Gone."

"I'm not surprised."

Wearing a calico dress that was tight and short, the girl shouldn't have been riding astride, Johnny was thinking as he dismounted at the porch. Tying the sorrel to a post, he took hold of the post to lift himself onto the gallery. Spurs making a racket, he walked down beside his uncle.

"Miss Rebecca, this is my sister's boy. Johnny McVay. He lives up in Wyoming."

Rebecca Casper inclined her head, looking from one to the other. "Yes," she said, "you all do favor. How do you like our valley, Johnny?"

"Well, it was all right till this morning."

The girl studied him intently. "How does it feel to kill a—an outlaw?"

"You got a father?"

Rebecca nodded.

"How would you feel if someone tried to stab him in the heart?"

"Awful. I'd feel like doing what you did to that old Blaine around there."

Sheriff Rodin cleared his throat. He was distantly watching the sunlit rangeland and far-off grazing cattle. "Sammy Lee will show up at your pa's place," he said, looking at the girl. "Tell him about Luther and Joe. Ask him if he heard Luther mention where him and Joe hid Barlow's money."

"I will."

Sheriff Rodin was talking for himself and the law, but he wasn't speaking for Johnny McVay. "Do you know where Sammy Lee might be right now?" Johnny asked.

Rebecca pursed her lips and tilted her head and said, "No."

"Sammy Lee hightailed it away from here on a horse of mine. If you see him before I do, you tell him to get that horse back to me as fast as he can. He can get it to me some way."

The girl gasped and stared. "You act like Sammy Lee stole it. He only borrowed it."

"He didn't ask if he could. And where I came from," Johnny said, "a horsethief is lower than a killer."

Rebecca's brown eyes flashed. "You'll get your horse back. And when you do, I hope you go home and stay there."

Johnny watched her coldly.

"Well, my lands!" she exclaimed, flushing. "If you got caught in the middle of a gunfight, wouldn't you have run? Wouldn't you have borrowed the first horse you came to?"

"No."

"Rebecca," the sheriff said, still trying to use honey instead of vinegar, "you tell Sammy Lee was I a young man again, I'd take you away from him. With a gal like you backing him, a man wouldn't have no worries at all."

"It's too late to take me away from him, Sheriff. I expect we'll be married by the time snow flies."

"As pretty as you are, Rebecca, I wouldn't be in no hurry to get married."

Rebecca darted a glance at Johnny McVay. Lifting the reins, she said, "Well, I'll go see if I can find Sammy Lee. No telling where he went, scared as he was."

"Reckon he's down at Saul's?"

"No. Him and Saul had a falling out." Reining the mare around, Rebecca headed along the road that went first one way and then another through fields of tall green cornstalks and towering, fire-blackened snags.

The dog trotted along behind.

Sheriff Rodin put on his hat and rubbed his chin whiskers. "I hope some man gets her that appreciates her. Sammy Lee sure won't."

Johnny McVay said, "I wouldn't have put it off. I'd have told her we believe that Sammy Lee was Blaine's pardner."

"Yeah, I know how you handle things. Joe's

lying in yonder at death's door right now. I've never knowed Joe to hurt anyone in his life. He was just drunk and mixed up. How are you going to pay him back for that?"

"He shouldn't have been here with these killers."

"He didn't know they was guilty."

"Well, he shouldn't have shot at me."

"Your clothes, I told you. You look as fancy as a Fiddlebacker. He couldn't see no badge on you. Those are Fiddleback cows grazing yonder."

Johnny McVay was silent.

In a less troubled tone, the sheriff said, "Go on and eat your breakfast and I'll be hooking up a team."

While Johnny was in the kitchen, a buggy rattled along the road. Coming into the hallway, he saw a man and woman and a boy driving toward Grief Hill; a farm family. They stared at the Dilts place as long as they could see it, and Johnny knew they had questioned Rebecca Casper.

Looking in on Joe Hooker, Johnny found him asleep.

Later, carrying his carbine, Johnny went out to open the corral gate. Some of the hens scratched and pecked until the last second and then took to legs and wings, squawking as though the horses' hoofs were purposely aimed at them.

Rodin wrapped the lines around the brake

handle. He lowered himself to the ground. Hitching up his gunbelt, he said, "My saddle scabbard's too big for your carbine. Why don't you lay it here in the wagon with these guns?"

Johnny did, but he said, "You ride your horse. I'll take the wagon in." He glanced at the sun. "Be hot as blazes on Joe without a sheet. Did you see one in the harness room?"

"Uh-huh."

Johnny found a set of bows and a nearly new wagon sheet. He and Rodin then rolled Blaine's body in the blanket and secured it with a quarter-inch rope. When they had the corpse straightened out in the box, they went into the house.

Joe Hooker was awake and feverish, features seamed with pain. He wasn't really an old man, Johnny observed, he just looked old. They carried him out to the wagon.

Sheriff Rodin said, "Joe, I'm purely sorry, but we've got to take Luther in, too."

"I'd just as soon ride with him as anybody," Hooker said. "Any whisky left?"

Johnny said, "Lots of it," and went to get the bottle. Climbing into the wagon, he lifted Hooker and gave him a swallow. Afterward he took a long swig himself.

Peering under the sheet, Rodin said, "Conscience bothering you?"

"Is that what it is?"

"Sure, conscience."

Sheriff Rodin jogged along behind the wagon until it was south of Little Goose Creek. The road then became so dusty he rode up. Reining over near the nigh front wheel, he said, "I'll ride on in, Johnny."

"All right."

"Care if I tell what happened—that you shot Joe and how come you to do it?"

"Tell it the way it was. What'll you say about Dilts?"

"What would you say?"

"In my mind, he was Luther Blaine's pardner."

The sheriff nodded. "Mine, too." He rode on.

There was low land to the west and south of the town, hills to the east. A ravine came down out of the hills to skirt the settlement on the north. Because of this, even though the *quebrada* was now bridged with iron and heavy timbers, no homes stood to the north, and the road was a lonely one.

The business part of Grief Hill began at the south end of the bridge. Modest homes had been constructed on the south and west, but the best residential section was on the hillsides to the east. The settlement had become "Grief Hill," Johnny had heard, because teamsters had cursed its mud in the early days, before the wet spots had been filled with rock.

With his sorrel at a jog-trot, Sheriff Rodin gradually pulled ahead.

A hawk soared and swooped over the hills, and the sun on Johnny's vest seemed unusually warm, since he hadn't stretched the sheet over the spring seat. Hubs knocking, doubletree and singletrees rattling, harness jingling, the bays pulled the wagon another hot mile. Their flanks were dark with sweat now, their collar pads being soaked with it. A lone tree stood beside the road within sight of the bridge, and when he reached it, Johnny pulled over into the shade. Half-hitching the lines around the brake handle, he got down to the ground. He tied the edges of the sheet back so that Joe Hooker would have more air. Hooker's eyes were open.

"How are you feeling, Joe?"

"Uh-huh. What's your name?"

"I asked you how you were feeling. I'm Johnny McVay, the man who shot you. Don't you remember?"

"Of course I remember. I may want to shoot you some day."

"No, you won't, Joe. Are you leaving anything undone, that I might finish for you? How about your quarrel with the Fiddleback?"

Hooker's eyes opened wider. "Yeah, sure. I want my daughter to have it."

"Wait a minute, now, Joe. Think hard so you'll give it to me straight."

"Hard? Uh-huh. I've got ten sections of land and a set of buildings Barlow ran me off of.

30

Accused me of squatting. I filed on it like he did his, and paid for it with scrip like he did his, and I've kept the taxes up on it. You make him—"

"He's dead, Joe."

"Dead. Uh-huh. Barlow and me, two ranches, two daughters. I lost all the way around, except I outlived him. Connie Clesson may be reasonable."

"Where's your daughter, Joe?"

"Treva? When her mother left me and married Eric Veblen, she took Eric's name. Treva went with her ma."

Johnny McVay frowned. "All right. What else, Joe?"

"I got Tom to see if she wanted me to will her the ranch, and she did. Help her get it. She wants to marry—" Hooker's voice trailed off. He was breathing heavily.

"Won't Veblen let her get married?"

A spasm of pain twisted Hooker's features. He raised up, face blue. "You swear it—that you'll help her to get—?"

Angrily Johnny McVay said, "Guess I have to." He watched Joe Hooker for a long while, but the man was either in a coma or dead.

Johnny's own face was set in grim lines when he pulled across the bridge and over toward the Hotel Tumbleweed where Rodin sat his saddle, talking with a man who stood behind the railing of the spacious veranda.

The man was Steve Fenwick, the town marshal. Others were there, and several came off the veranda to peer under the sheet. One man climbed up, gently moved the blanket-wrapped body, then looked at Joe Hooker.

"Oscar," he said, "you're mistaken about Joe. He's dead as a doornail."

"Well, he was alive when I left him," Rodin said. He passed his gaze over the men behind the railing. "One of you fellers go and tell Pablo Cardoza I need him."

Johnny McVay said, "Drive on, Uncle Oscar?"

"Uh-huh. But you'd better stop at the drugstore, so the doc can look at Joe. He might not be dead."

Johnny said glumly, "Yes, he is, too," and slapped the bays with the lines.

A saddle and harness shop stood directly across from the hotel. Taking the wagon south along the main thoroughfare, Johnny passed the public square and courthouse, on the hotel side. Business structures stood across from it. The next intersection was the center of town. A dug well lined with rock to a high curb centered the intersection. A flume to dump the water in that was drawn for the horse trough slanted from the curb. Northeast from it was the drugstore, with the doctor's office in the rear. Pulling over in front, Johnny McVay got down.

Following the wagon, Sheriff Rodin dismounted and tied his sorrel to the hitch rack, and he saw Pablo Cardoza angling across the square.

When the Mexican came up, Rodin said to him, "Pablo, when Doc Mueller gets through here, you take this wagon on over to the hardware store. Don't help them unload it; they'll get paid for it. This is Dilts's wagon and team. Feed and water them bays and rub them down, and take them home. Lead a bronc to ride back."

"*Si, senor.*"

Being busy with a patient, Doctor Mueller didn't come out with the sheriff at once.

Getting his carbine from the wagon, Johnny stood on the boardwalk, rifle clamped under an arm while he rolled a cigarette.

Marshal Fenwick, hat pushed back from his florid face, came over to him and braced a boot on the hitching rail beside him. "Did you hear about Jay Minch?"

"Minch? Who's he?"

"A dealer at Eric Veblen's place—or he *was* a dealer. When Minch showed up this morning, Eric got into a fuss with him and killed him."

"What were they fussing over?"

"Money. Minch was in on robbing and killing Barlow Clesson. He dealt the crooked cards."

"Barlow's winnings were really Eric's, then. Guess Eric didn't like being made a sucker of."

"He sure didn't like something," the marshal said. "Eric's a right prideful man. He's always kept the Silver Saddle games straight."

Johnny blew ash off his cigarette. "Wade and Uncle Oscar both gone, you had to arrest him without help, didn't you?"

A short-statured man, the marshal turned to sit on the rail. "I didn't arrest him. I wanted to ask Oscar what to do about it."

"What did he say?"

"He said, 'Let's not worry about it right now, Steve.'" The marshal squinted. "Johnny, you must have known Minch. He knew you."

Johnny shook his head.

"I found a newspaper in his room with a piece about you in it."

Johnny showed increasing interest. "I'd like to see it."

"It'll be there. I put a padlock on Minch's door, figuring Oscar would want to handle things himself."

A man coming out of the drugstore said, "Eric told me you found a cocked derringer in Minch's fist, Steve."

Marshal Fenwick stared a moment, florid features paling. "Uh-huh. Minch would have downed Eric if Eric had been a shade slower—that's what you want me to say, ain't it? You know danged well I never found no derringer!"

Owen Tyndale smiled. Of medium height, he carried himself with military bearing. Under a silk stovepipe hat, his hair was silver as was his mustache. Even at this hot afternoon hour, he appeared comfortable. His boots had been recently polished. His trousers and coat were of fine broadcloth, and he was wearing a ruffled shirt with a string tie.

Looking at Johnny McVay, he said, "Steve's easily riled."

"Maybe he doesn't like jokes about something that's that serious. I wouldn't."

The attorney sobered. "I know how you feel, Johnny." He changed the subject. "The Sioux Indians are making it rough on you Wyoming people, aren't they?"

"Yes, sir. They're depredating quite a bit."

The marshal, the attorney and Johnny McVay shifted their interest to the drugstore then, as Sheriff Rodin and Doctor Mueller emerged.

Mueller's examination was brief.

Joe Hooker was indeed dead, and for a moment Johnny kept his gaze on the sidewalk, speculating as to how it would be like when he faced Joe's daughter, a chore he had to do soon.

Sheriff Rodin glanced around. "Where did Pablo get off to?"

"*Aqui, senor.*" The Mexican came around the wagon looking at the sheriff questioningly. Rodin nodded. Pablo climbed up to the seat and drove the bays across the intersection.

Lawyer Tyndale walked north along the boardwalk.

Sheriff Rodin said, "Johnny, water my sorrel,

will you?" and he cut across the street to the plaza, headed for his office.

Squaring around with his florid visage troubled, Marshal Fenwick said, "Wait a minute, Johnny. What would you do about that Philadelphia shyster, if you was me?"

"I don't understand what you mean."

"Would you stretch the truth a little to help Eric Veblen out of a jam?"

Johnny shook his head. "Eric's not in any jam. If they needed your help, Steve, that lawyer wouldn't be rawhiding you and grinning like a possum eating *chapotes*."

The marshal nodded slowly. There was a vague look in his eyes, but he said nothing further. He went across the street to the funeral parlor.

Vaulting over the hitch rail, Johnny laid the carbine on the sidewalk and loosened the sorrel's cinches. He got the gun and took the horse to the trough and drew water to replace that which the sorrel had drunk, then he tied the sorrel in front of the drugstore again. Pablo was turning the wagon around in the street now, the two bodies having been carried into the funeral parlor. Johnny went back to the well, quenching his own thirst and divesting himself of sweat and dust.

South along this street stood the Emporium and the post office. Beyond that was a freighter's wagon yard and corrals. Modest homes occupied the area across from the freighter's layout, one of which was Deputy Smollet's. Between it and the bank on the corner was the town's only restaurant.

Johnny McVay dragged his spurs toward the restaurant.

It was a narrow building, having only a counter and stools. Of the three vacant stools, Johnny chose the one in the center.

The waiter had on an apron, an undershirt and a paper cap. Hard of hearing, he leaned over the counter to take Johnny's order for the regular dinner. Johnny took roast beef and waited, amid the smells and clatter.

Before he was served two men entered the restaurant together and took the stools on either side of him. They were stony-featured men who had hit town after a lengthy absence, because they had just come from the barbershop with fresh shaves, haircuts and baths. Under buckskin vests, they had on new shirts. Their neckerchiefs were new and bright, as were their Levi's.

The man on the right had two Charter-oak Colts strapped around him, and the grips of the gun nearer Johnny had been notched. The man was tall and thin-faced, and his gray eyes had a way of appearing immovable in their sockets.

The man on the left was heavyset and light complexioned. Leaning forward to send his voice past Johnny McVay, he said, "Let's see what he looks like before we ride out, Clete."

Clete said, "Well."

Glancing from side to side, Johnny said, "If you fellows are together, let me change stools with one of you."

Clete said, "Keep your seat." He gave Johnny another direct look. Brows lifting the least bit, he said to his partner, "This could be him, right here, Vic."

"Could be who?" Johnny asked. His tone held a slight challenge.

"Oscar Rodin's nephew. You fit the description."

"Uh-huh."

"I'm Clete Maisie. He's Vic McVickers. We're Fiddleback. How come you didn't tally that clodhopper, too?"

"Well, there was some doubt about him. Your boss hadn't identified him. I didn't even know Luther Blaine by sight. As I told my uncle, I was thinking of myself, not of enforcing the law, or I wouldn't have shot Joe Hooker."

After a silence, Maisie said, "I almost shot Joe once, too, but somehow I felt sorry for him. He spent his whole life, seems like, *almost* amounting to something."

Johnny McVay's meal came, and as the waiter moved the side dishes from tray to counter, Maisie and McVickers both looked at the food appreciatively. Both ordered the same.

Johnny said then, "Wade Smollet rode out to

the Fiddleback, taking word to Miss Connie. You fellows must have met him."

"We rode down from the south," Maisie said. "Hogarth sent us to help gather a herd that's leaving the valley. Man who owned it was caught mavericking."

"Cut out any of yours this time?"

"No," Maisie said, "the herd was clean."

A little later Johnny McVay paid for his meal and went out, noticing that Clete Maisie's right-hand six-shooter, as opposed to his other one, had not been notched.

CHAPTER III

Johnny McVay, with a full stomach, felt better physically, but he was still out of sorts with the world. He still had Joe Hooker's daughter to face. He smoked an after-dinner cigarette standing on the bank corner, watching the group at the public well. Over near the courthouse, a larger group stood around the horseshoe game, which generally continued till dark. Sometimes a couple of experts, teamed up, would hold forth all day long, and it wasn't a game for children. Often the bet was a thousand dollars. Owen Tyndale was an onlooker there now.

Johnny wanted to see him. Crossing the street and passing into the shade of the trees on the square, Johnny started toward the attorney but went only halfway because he caught Tyndale's attention and gestured.

Leaning against a tree bole when the attorney reached him, Johnny said, "You're Veblen's lawyer. You know Treva, old Joe Hooker's daughter, too, I reckon."

Tyndale reset his tall silk hat. His eyes were narrowed. "You want to speak with her about Joe?"

"Could you arrange it?"

"I'll have to see Eric Veblen first."

Johnny watched Tyndale's silver-mustached face intently. "Is she worth the trouble that Joe tried to saddle me with?"

Tyndale's features hardened. He said coldly, "You'll have to judge that for yourself."

Johnny put a hand in his pocket. "I will. How much for this consultation?"

"Don't be sarcastic, Johnny."

Johnny McVay took his hand out of his pocket. "Is her mother dead?"

"Yes."

Johnny then explained all that had happened on Little Goose Creek and along the road when he had brought the wagon in.

Afterward, Tyndale said, "Treva knows only what folks have told her. She was just a baby when her mother married Eric. He told her his side of it. He said he had to, so she would understand why she was able to lead him around by the nose."

Johnny glanced away for a moment. "Joe mentioned someone named Tom. Who's he?"

"Tom Saxon. He just comes and goes. His older brother bought Joe's cattle when Tom was a boy, and Tom's been coming here ever since."

"Acquainted with Treva?"

"With nearly everyone. You offered to pay me—I'll give you some advice free. Too much water has run under the bridge for you to do anything with Joe's place. The Fiddleback will never stand for it, and now that Connie has full charge out there, running the spread alone, she'll have public sympathy behind her. Barlow never did have that."

"The Fiddleback may stand more from me than you think, Mr. Tyndale. Arrange for me to meet Treva."

"I'll go see Eric now," Tyndale said, and they separated, the attorney walking northeast, Johnny going northwest, jingling his spurs toward the courthouse.

The stoop of the two-story masonry building was a fine place to sit and whittle, and several nesters were doing that now. Two range-clad men stood in front of the doorway. At the moment, Johnny McVay didn't feel like walking around them. He poked his carbine forward and edged between them, and one protested profanely.

Just inside the doorway, Johnny McVay turned. "You really want trouble?"

Both men were belted with sixguns, but under battered hats the features of both were relaxed. The man who'd sworn—rough-hewn and grizzled—said, "That's what I thought I wanted, but I see now I was mistaken."

The other was slender and swarthy, dark-eyed. "What we really want, mister, is two riding jobs. We don't care where."

"Are you afraid of the Fiddleback?"

43

The grizzled man said, "That depends. We wouldn't blot their brand."

Johnny told who he was and what he hoped to do. The grizzled man was Vern Masefield; the other, Pete Creighton. They had heard about Blaine and Hooker and Clesson. Because of the nearby nesters, Sammy Lee Dilts wasn't mentioned. Having been fleeced by the crooked tinhorn, Minch, they were Veblen's friends for life. Treva was a fine-looking girl, and if she wanted to buck Connie Clesson the way Joe had fought her father, Barlow, they would ride for Treva.

"I don't know how many hands I'll hire," Johnny said, "or how many horses I'll buy. We'll drive a bunch out with us, though, just to see if we can stick."

Masefield said, "Do you want us to keep an eye out for some broncs?"

"You could. Here, I'll give you some money, and you can make a payment on them to bind the bargain, if you find any."

Thrusting a hand into his pocket, Johnny brought out a roll of bills. He didn't know which man to offer it to.

Creighton said, "Vern's older and knows more. Give it to him."

The grizzled rider took the money. "Any other orders?"

"I can't think of any. I've got a room at the

hotel, if something comes up you want to ask me about." And Johnny went on upstairs.

Most of the upper floor was occupied by judges' chambers, council rooms and offices. The cell block was in the rear. Sheriff Rodin's office was in the southeast corner, and Johnny found him standing at a south window. Hearing Johnny, he turned around.

"What did you do with my sorrel?"

"Tied him in the same place. Can't you see it?"

"Trees are too thick. That's all right."

Johnny crossed the room to the gun rack in the corner. "I'll put my carbine here till I get my horse and saddle back."

"Uh-huh. You say Wells Fargo give you that?"

"I helped smoke up some outlaws for them. Got a treasure chest back. They gave us all new repeaters."

"Uh-huh. What was you talking with Owen Tyndale about?"

"About Joe's daughter. Why didn't you tell me who she was?"

"I thought you already knowed." The sheriff walked over to the roll-top desk and sank into his swivel chair. "I reckon Joe filled your ear full of talk about his ranch. Better not mess with it. Them Fiddleback men are hostile."

Johnny didn't want to talk about that. He said, "When are you going to arrest Eric Veblen for killing Minch?"

"I ain't."

"Well, when is the marshal going to?"

"Steve ain't, either. Eric done this here town, and valley too, a favor when he plugged Minch."

"Maybe so, but the law is the law, Uncle Oscar."

"*And* so is Uncle Oscar. Boy, your uncle is all the law there is, hereabouts."

"You make me tired," Johnny said. He walked out of the office. He went downstairs, edged among the men on the stoop and met Tyndale, who was on his way up.

"Eric said it would be all right. Treva's coming downtown, going to meet him at the Emporium, and he said he would tell her to have supper ready for us at his house. How's that?"

"Suits me fine. I'll return the favor. My stepfather owns the Crescent Lazy Two, on the Laramie Plains. Ever up there, why, drop in on them. If you like real frontier eating, go out to the cookshack and try some of Shoo-fly Flynn's—" Johnny broke off. He snapped his fingers. "I was going to say, try some of Shoo-fly Flynn's buffalo hump ribs and beaver tail, but he's not there any more."

Tyndale said, "I don't like beaver tail; it's too much like fat pork. Just plain barnyard chicken's my dish."

"Meat's meat."

"Yes, I know," Tyndale said. "Where will you be at eight o'clock?"

"At the hotel."

"I'll bring my buggy around and pick you up," the attorney said.

Freshly shaved and bathed, Johnny was on the hotel veranda when he saw the red-wheeled rig swing around the corner near the public well. Tyndale came on and passed the hotel to make a turn at the end of the bridge; then he pulled over near the hotel steps.

Johnny met him even as he brought the grays to a stop and stepped up to sit beside him.

Shadows stretched everywhere now, and the daytime bustle of Grief Hill had subsided. Tyndale tooled the dappled horses back to the main intersection. He made a turn around the well and headed up the street between the drugstore and the hardware store.

The attorney said, "Eric doesn't want you to mention Joe's plans to her tonight. We'll just make it a social call."

"Why?"

"Treva would be at a disadvantage. You'll have to get together on neutral ground to discuss her affairs. She and Eric don't always see eye to eye."

"I don't quite savvy, Mr. Tyndale."

"She won't trust you."

After a silence, Johnny said, "Eric and I are sort of on the same side."

"The Fiddleback side," Tyndale said.

"Why did Eric kill Minch?"

"Eric thought that Minch's crooked deal had ruined the Silver Saddle. He couldn't shoulder the hurt and disappointment. He knew Minch was no good, but trusted him, anyway, and got betrayed. They quarreled. Several saw and heard it but I didn't get all the details."

Johnny was silent.

Tyndale said, "Eric is in the clear. Bedford Polk is waiting now for a telegram that will clear him."

"Back-trailing Minch?"

"Yes," Tyndale said. "Johnny, if you're expecting to find Treva in mourning, I'd better tell you now you won't find her that way."

"Well, that's in her favor. She's no hypocrite."

There was only one street of importance on the bench. After Tyndale had reined the dappled grays onto it, he indicated a well-kept residence on the right.

"That's my home. Want to stop for a drink? Treva won't serve any liquor."

"If she won't serve it, I don't want her to smell it on me."

Only one row of houses spaced far apart nestled against the rounded hillsides. This being open range, all were enclosed by fences of wood or vines or shrubbery. Lamps had been lighted in most of them. With the buggy rolling north, Johnny had a view of the timber which marked the windings of Little Goose Creek. The vista extended across shadowy rangeland for miles. The land that Joe Hooker had owned was far to the northwest. The headquarters locations of other ranches, being lamplighted, were visible off yonder, but the spurs of the distant mountain formed an indistinct, solid wall. Conversely, the mountain summits were boldly defined, the sky in the west being light.

"Hold these a moment, Johnny."

Coming out of his landscape reverie, Johnny didn't take the lines. He sprang from the buggy, spurs jingling, saying, "I'll do it."

Tyndale had stopped at a gate in a whitewashed stake-and-rider fence. Swinging the gate open, Johnny saw that this driveway led past the Veblen home, a two-story house, to its carriage house and stables. Lamplighted windows revealed the carriage house had living quarters above it. The main house had a gallery across the front and along the south side. When Johnny got back into the buggy, the attorney drove up to the south side of the house and stopped in lamplight which came from a crosswise hall.

A denim-clad oldster whom Tyndale called Ross took a bit ring and led the team and buggy on into the barnlot.

Treva stood on the porch but not directly in the

shaft of light. "Go right in, Owen. You two make yourselves at home."

When all three had entered the lighted hallway, Tyndale and the younger man turned to face her, hats in hand. She wasn't as old as Johnny. Tall, she had eyes so dark and hair of such a black sheen it almost hurt you to look at her. Her hair wasn't curly or wavy, either; it bent around her pretty head just the way Johnny thought it should. Her dress was of dark satin with white cuffs, a white leather belt and a stand-up white collar. Johnny could see a tiny gold chain at her throat, but the rest of it, undoubtedly a locket, was on the inside. She'd been wearing a frilly apron but had removed it to greet her guests.

The attorney introduced Johnny.

Treva held out her hands. "I'll take your hats. Owen, you two go on to the parlor. Mrs. Ross wanted me to bake the biscuits. Dinner will soon be ready. Johnny, do you like fried chicken? We have stuffed *chuletas*, too."

Somewhere in the room nearby grease was hissing and sizzling, and Johnny was enjoying mouth-watering odors. He smiled and said, "Meat's meat."

Tyndale led the way into another hall, and when they passed the door of the dining room, Johnny saw a shimmering chandelier above a table resplendent with a fine cloth and old silver, delicate china and fragile glassware.

Well, Johnny had learned one thing about her. She had been back East among the factory workers, because she had called tonight's meal dinner.

Treva followed them and turned into a darkened room opposite the dining room to deposit the hats, while the two men continued on toward the parlor.

The night was as black except for the starshine when Johnny closed the gate behind the buggy and rejoined the attorney on the cushioned seat. The dappled grays then sought to break into a trot. Tyndale held them to an amble.

"Why so silent, Johnny?"

"Just thinking. Treva said she had been home a year. Home from where?"

"From Baltimore, Maryland. Eric sent her to a school for young females." The attorney paused and said, "She sure likes you, Johnny."

"That'll make it easier."

The attorney walked the grays all the way down the slope, and they reached the center of town. There was light in the sheriff's office. At the drugstore corner, Johnny said, "I'll get out here. Tell Treva I enjoyed the dinner, and I want to see her again soon. I told her once, but it won't hurt to tell her again."

"Now that you're acquainted with her," Tyndale said, in parting, "you can talk with her anytime."

Johnny stood there until the attorney had started back up the slope, the red-wheeled rig rattling away in a smelly cloud of dust.

It was hours till stage time, but Wells Fargo & Company's express office was open, the hotel veranda and lobby being ablaze with light. Lanterns shone at the company barns. Light spilled also from Veblen's Silver Saddle Saloon. Except for those places, Grief Hill was silent and dark.

Crossing onto the plaza, Johnny headed for the courthouse.

Sheriff Rodin had no jailer. He and Deputy Smollet handled everything, paper work and law enforcement, and took turns, month about, keeping the office open at night.

This was the sheriff's month for night work. He would have been here regardless, however. After the long ride, Wade Smollet would have been too tired, and Connie Clesson, wanting a first-hand account of the gunfight on Little Goose Creek, would have rousted Rodin out anyway.

When Johnny McVay reached the courthouse stoop, he came to a sudden stop at the tinkle of familiar spurs. Presently then, silhouetted dimly, Deputy Wade Smollet came around the northeast corner of the building. Johnny leaned against the stoop wall and waited.

When Smollet's round face was near, Johnny said, "Just getting in."

The deputy came upon the stoop. "Yeah. What happened down the creek?"

"We didn't take any prisoners."

"Somebody said you killed Joe Hooker."

"Did somebody tell you why?"

The deputy let a couple of seconds go by. "Oscar should have told you about Joe. He's been living with Saul Delbert, and was liable to show up at Sammy Lee Dilts's place any time."

"Why didn't you tell me?"

"I didn't think of it."

"Well, it's too late now," Johnny said. "Did the Clesson girl come with you?"

"Yeah, her and two of the hands. Some of the Fiddleback outfit was already here. One of them rode home a little while after I got there."

"Wasn't really necessary for you to go."

"Well, Oscar wants to keep on friendly terms with them," the deputy said, and entered the building. He and Johnny went upstairs to find the sheriff sleeping in his swivel chair, steel-rimmed spectacles still on his nose and a newspaper crumpled on his lap. Their noisy entrance aroused him. He straightened around and blinked.

"Miss Connie come with you?"

The deputy nodded. "But she won't be up here tonight. They stopped at the hotel, and I put their broncs in our stable."

Sheriff Rodin said, "Uh-huh."

"Oscar, could Luther have been lying, you reckon? It's possible Joe was his pardner."

"Ain't, either. Sammy Lee was his pardner. Make no mistake about that, Wade."

The deputy toed a chair around and slumped down dispiritedly.

Sheriff Rodin said, "Your job, Wade, after you get some sleep, will be to go down there and keep an eye on that nester settlement. Collar Sammy Lee. But he may light a shuck, having that whole nine thousand dollars."

"I figure he will. He'll head for The Nations, if he's guilty."

"Don't say '*if* he's guilty.' Confound it, they ain't any doubt about it."

"And he'll take Rebecca Casper with him," the deputy continued.

"Uh-huh. And his dog. A man's woman and his dog is always the last to quit him."

Smollet said, "A man's dog is the loyalest."

"Well," the sheriff said, "you won't ever have to worry about such things as wives, Wade. You've got the best woman a man ever had."

Deputy Smollet made no comment. "Them fellers at the express office said Eric plugged his houseman."

Sheriff Rodin gave a slight nod.

"Arrested him?"

"No. Bedford Polk said not to."

"Well, what he says, goes." Deputy Smollet

surveyed the sheriff. "You look plumb tuckered out, yourself, Oscar. Want me to take over for the rest of the night?"

"No. Go on home and get some sleep, so you can head back down Little Goose Creek. Johnny, you get gone, too. Nothing you can do around here."

A bright moon was showing above the line of business structures when Johnny and the deputy came out upon the stoop.

"See you later, Wade."

"Yeah. *Buenos noches*, Johnny."

Later, Johnny wished he'd said *Vaya con Dios* or something.

CHAPTER IV

The next day, on his hands and knees in the gambler's hotel room, Marshal Fenwick was saying, "They're telling around I found some money stashed here. That ain't so. Sure, Eric paid him good wages, and he didn't have any bank account. But, by thunder, I ought to know what I found."

It was a valise that the marshal got from under the bed. The lock had been forced.

"Bedford Polk kept the keys." Getting a newspaper, the marshal stood up and passed it to Johnny McVay. Pointing, he said, "There it is; he marked it."

It was an item about Johnny McVay's leaving on a trip to Texas to visit his mother's brother.

When Johnny raised his eyes, the marshal said, "If Minch didn't know you, he knowed all about you. Didn't he ever mention it to you?"

"I never even saw him in my life," Johnny said. He looked at the bag. "What else is in there?"

Marshal Fenwick swung the valise onto the bed and turned it upside-down to spill its contents.

Among other things there were a shoulder holster and short-barreled revolver, a two-shot .41 derringer with a wrist clip, a heavy gold watch and chain, an assortment of jewelry and

57

a sheaf of newspapers. About a dozen letters with envelopes postmarked Rawlins, Wyoming Territory.

Picking up one of these, Johnny glanced over the handwriting. Frowning, he started at the beginning and read the letter through. He rolled and lit a cigarette and then read more of the letters. He perused the newspapers. Dropping his cigarette into a saucer on the bureau, he asked the marshal, "Have you read this stuff?"

Marshal Fenwick shook his head. "Just that piece he marked."

Johnny handed him a letter. "Read that one."

The florid badge-toter started on the text, lips forming the words. He struggled through half of it and paused to ask, "Who is she?"

"A dance-hall girl."

"He's been sending her his money. No wonder I couldn't find none here."

"Blackmail," Johnny said. "He was paying her to keep her mouth shut concerning his whereabouts. He thought she loved him. He let her know where he'd run to, then she got her hooks into him."

Marshal Fenwick tossed the missive onto the pile. "If Minch was still alive and over there in the Silver Saddle dealing cards, I'd march right out of here and plug him through the gizzard. Murdered his wife."

"No doubt about it."

Marshal Fenwick read a couple of the newspaper accounts. "Name was really Minch Jayson."

"Jayson, yes. Wasn't any penitentiary in Wyoming Territory, and they had to take him back to Rock Island, Illinois. He escaped before they got him there."

Marshal Fenwick kept searching. Folded between the pages of a book, he found a dodger.

"Listen to this, Johnny. A thousand dollars reward, for capture and delivery to Wyoming attorney-general's office . . ."

Johnny glanced over Fenwick's shoulder.

The marshal said, "What makes a man gather up stuff like this and keep it with him, I've never been able to figure. Looks like he would want to get shut of it as fast as he could."

Johnny said, "Maybe he considered it insurance. If he had gotten into hanging trouble hereabouts, he could have proved himself worth the thousand dollars' bounty. Not many men would have killed him. They would have taken him back to Wyoming, maybe even received travel money. Minch would have gained time and might have escaped again."

An odd expression on his florid countenance, the marshal kept his lips tight for a long while. Finally he said sheepishly, "Them fellers have been making a fool out of me, especially that Philadelphia lawyer."

"It looks that way."

"Wonder who'll get the reward money?"

"If there is any, why don't you claim it, or part of it?"

"Yeah, why not?" the marshal said. "I had more to do with it than anybody, excepting Eric. Are you through here, Johnny?"

"I came with you."

"I'm ready to go." Chucking Minch's belongings back into the bag, the marshal clamped it under an arm. He restrained himself descending the stairs, but he hurried across the lobby, impatient to reach Owen Tyndale's office.

Johnny McVay paused on the hotel veranda. A nester wagon was rattling the timbers of the bridge, menfolks holding down the spring seat, womenfolks in cane-bottomed chairs behind them, black parasols raised against the sun. There were other wagons on the square, unharnessed teams tethered to rear wheels where they could munch the hay from the boxes. Sodbusters and cowhands, too, were loafing in the shade roundabout.

Going on past the traffic jam at the well, Johnny entered the bank.

Earlier in the morning, he'd mailed a letter back home to the Crescent Lazy 2, telling the prospects of his locating in this valley. Having sold off a Wyoming herd to pay a debt, he had banked a few dollars, too. Now he arranged for transfer of his funds from a Cheyenne bank to the local institution. He told himself if he needed more, he would borrow it from his ma and step-father.

When he left the bank, he went to the hardware store, hunted up the funeral director and paid for the best casket and clothes available for Joe Hooker.

"Be sure you don't put a hatchet in that coffin," Johnny said. He left the undertaker staring open mouthed.

Johnny crossed the street to the drugstore and intended to cut across the plaza to the county corral, but noticing the silver-haired attorney among a group on the corner, Johnny joined him.

"Was Marshal Fenwick pretty upset?" Johnny asked.

"Yes, yes indeed." The lawyer smiled. "I'll make it right with him."

Near the attorney was a young man, clean-shaven and of determined mien. He wore a frock coat and a dark tie with a white shirt, and had a forelock of black hair showing beneath a Mormon-style hat.

The attorney said to him, "Brother Phillips, this is Johnny McVay, the sheriff's nephew."

The Reverend Phillips extended a hand.

Johnny took it and said, "I was thinking of you. I want you to preach Joe Hooker's funeral."

"Miss Veblen has already mentioned it to me."

Tyndale said, "Eric and Treva, Brother Phillips and I are going together. We'll have room for you."

"I'll go horseback," Johnny said. "I paid for the casket and clothes and burial plot."

"You didn't need to. Eric would have done it."

Johnny was frowning when he took leave of Tyndale and Phillips. He considered having a talk with the saloonkeeper now, because he had to find out for himself what Veblen thought about Joe Hooker. Eric Veblen would have a big say in whatever Treva did about the ranch, regardless of Tyndale's statement to the contrary. Johnny was in doubt about Treva but not about himself. He intended to move onto the ranch, thus corralling nine points of the law, and palaver later.

The Silver Saddle was straight ahead.

Johnny had barely passed the milliner and dressmaker's shop, however, when he heard his name. When he turned back, the girl said, "You are Johnny McVay, aren't you?"

"Yes, ma'am," he said. He doffed his Stetson.

"I want to thank you for bringing in those men who killed my father."

Wearing dainty boots and spurs, a doeskin riding skirt and a blue satin blouse, she was a couple of years younger than Johnny. Her mouth was firm and quite pretty. Her features were suntanned. A chin strap that didn't touch her chin swung from her hat. Her light blonde hair was snipped close and thick, and her dark eyes bore evidence of violent weeping.

Johnny's own face was wry. "Miss Connie, we only got one of them."

"Two, I thought."

"Well, Joe Hooker."

"Well, Johnny, don't you worry one bit about it. If he didn't do it, it wasn't because he didn't want to."

"But a man ought not to be buried just for wanting, Connie."

She averted her gaze. After a moment her eyes came back to his, and she said, "We're going to take Dad home for burial. Would you like to go with us?"

"It's too far out there, Connie."

Apparently she desired to talk further, but other women were watching a few feet away, inside the dressmaker's shop. Managing a brief smile, she said, "Be seeing you," and turned away, going toward the drugstore.

Johnny put on his hat. He wanted to stand there and gawk, liking the way Connie moved, but he couldn't afford to. He walked north.

He passed the Valley Dry Goods and reached the saloon, but now he had changed his plans. He wouldn't talk with Veblen just yet. Continuing on, he crossed the side street to a smaller building opposite the hotel. A fine-looking papier-mâché horse on casters, saddled and bridled, was displayed on the porch of this establishment.

The blanket and bridle suited Johnny, but the kak, even though properly rigged, wasn't exactly what he wanted. He bought it anyway and left an order with the proprietor for a custom-made one.

He had no idea when he would recover the blaze-faced black gelding and that gear. Probably never, if Sammy Lee Dilts had lit out for The Nations.

He would buy a horse from the public stable, whose owner had a high-headed gray Johnny liked. It took quite a while to make the deal, and then he paid more than he should have. Intending to ride bareback down the street for the new saddle, Johnny put a rope *bozal* on the gray and led him out of the corral.

Swarthy Pete Creighton and grizzled Vern Masefield emerged from the stable office while Johnny was still at the gate. "Johnny," Masefield said, "you won't like this, but Pete and me lost that money you gave us. Playing poker."

Johnny McVay's blond features showed quick and angry resentment. He controlled it, though, and asked, "Want some more?"

"I reckon. If you still expect us to get a remuda together."

Johnny swung astride the gray. "I'll have to go to the bank and draw it."

Masefield and Creighton exchanged glances.

Masefield said then, "What really went with it, Johnny—we owed a few bills we just couldn't let ride any longer. You take it out of our pay."

The Silver Saddle Saloon, Johnny McVay had learned, was the oldest business establishment in the valley. It had opened for business in a tent when Texas was a republic, its bar then being wagon sideboards placed atop whisky barrels. Buffalo hunters, mustangers, *comancheros*, bullwhackers, teamsters and scouting parties of Rangers had been the principal customers.

When Eric Veblen bought it, it was a box-and-batten structure with a false front. A little later, he spruced it up a little and employed percentage girls. It was now a handsome building two-stories high with a mezzanine.

The Silver Saddle still enjoyed the patronage of the old days, except for the Rangers, and to this had been added that of cowboys from the ranches to the south and west, sodbusters from the lower reaches of Little Goose Creek, and emigrants and drummers as well as local business and professional men and public servants.

At an early morning hour Johnny McVay pushed through the batwing swinging doors.

Veblen's office was on the mezzanine. The red-curtained booths were up there too, on either side, but percentage girls were no longer employed.

Only men were in sight downstairs, six of them.

One was the white-aproned bartender. Another was the walrus-mustached old swamper, who was busy with a garden rake, combing trash and coins out of the sawdust among the covered gambling layouts.

Two others were Wells Fargo men, one at the bar, one at the piano. Upon Johnny McVay's entrance, the man at the piano, playing with one finger, voiced, "Get along little doggies," and Johnny lifted a hand at him.

Johnny also noticed Bedford Polk, the county attorney. Polk had seen better days. Having now resigned himself to rough-handed and sometimes devious frontier justice, however, he had turned his office into a sinecure. He was a portly man, dressed in broadcloth. An ancient stovepipe hat covered his bald head. A bristly mustache adorned his lip, and stiff brows jutted over his crowsfooted eyes.

Beside him was a man Johnny had never seen before.

Wide across the shoulders and thick through the chest, this man had on a kipskin vest. Johnny glanced at his ivory-handled six-shooter. A thick mane of tawny hair swung below his diamondback-banded hat. His features were probably considered handsome by women, but Johnny McVay instinctively resented them as being just a mite too handsome.

Johnny McVay, accustomed to Mormondistilled valley tan, would just as lief have had his drink out of the barrel at two bits a shot, but Bedford Polk's private bottle came sliding along the bar to meet him as he bellied up.

Polk took no further notice of Johnny.

Resuming his conversation with the tawny-haired man, he said, "If you cleared nine dollars a head and trailed three thousand head, you brought back twenty-seven thousand dollars. Call it luck if you want to, but I call it brains."

The tawny-haired man had an intent, listening expression, but he kept silent.

Polk said, "Why don't you settle down now?"

"I may do that, Bedford." Having noticed the private bottle exchange, the tawny-haired man lowered his voice. "Who is he?"

"The sheriff's nephew." Polk glanced sidewise. "Johnny, this—"

The tawny-haired man didn't wait for Polk to finish. He walked around to confront Johnny McVay with rank hostility.

"I thought you were. You're the kid who killed Joe Hooker."

Whisky glass in his left hand, Johnny said, "Don't crowd me till you sober up, fellow."

"The way I heard it, you killed Joe just for being there with Blaine and Dilts. What kind of law enforcement is that? You don't even belong here."

"Anywhere I've got kinfolks, I belong."

The man's handsome face was bitter. "I felt sorry for that old man, losing his wife to Eric and his ranch to Barlow Clesson."

Bedford Polk said, "Be careful, Tom. Eric's in his office."

Tom Saxon glanced around furiously. "You think I'm another tinhorn who's scared of him?"

"Well, it's not right to wash your dirty linen in public. Some of it's his."

Johnny downed the whisky and put the glass on the bar. He laid down a quarter for the bartender. He reached for the makings, filled a paper and tucked the sack back in his vest.

"Joe Hooker bucked the meanest outfit in this valley for years," Saxon said, "and then he was gunned down by a kid tagging around after his badge-toting uncle. It just doesn't make sense."

"You just want to quarrel. You don't want to fight."

Eyes wide and glinting, mouth flattened, Saxon lunged forward. He grabbed a handful of Johnny's shirt and vest, jerking him forward. Johnny dropped his cigarette, but he offered no resistance.

Saxon said nothing.

Presently he turned loose of Johnny's clothing and stepped back.

Johnny's gunhand went down and came up. He didn't thumb the hammer. He brought the barrel of the Remington up under Tom Saxon's chin.

Saxon threw his arms wide and reeled backward, Polk making room for him. Johnny struck Saxon on the shoulder. He brought the sixgun flat to his own chest and then slapped Saxon alongside the head. Saxon went down.

Holstering the gun, Johnny turned back to the bar. He poured another drink and slid the bottle back to its owner.

Polk said, "I'll have another one myself, Johnny. I need it."

"That's pretty good stuff," Johnny said. "I'll buy a bottle when you run out."

Saxon had climbed to his feet. Holding to the bar to steady himself, he reset his hat and began brushing his clothes.

He looked at Johnny McVay. "Drunker than I thought."

"I don't hold it against you."

"They said you told them Joe was shooting at you. I didn't believe it then, but I do now."

"Joe thought I was Fiddleback," Johnny said. He went toward the stairway then.

CHAPTER V

The staircase with polished newelposts and bannisters filled the center of the saloon in the rear. The mezzanine was railed, and Eric Veblen had been standing there with hands on the rail, watching events below, since he'd heard Polk caution Saxon. He turned away when Johnny McVay left the bar.

Reaching the landing, Johnny was ten feet from the door of the office, and the door was open. A deep-pile rug covered the floor and a massive walnut desk faced the doorway.

The saloonkeeper was seated in a high-back upholstered swivel chair. Veblen, at fifty, was now graying. He was well dressed in broadcloth clothing tailored for his shape, but he was a fat man nevertheless, a heavily jowled man who was an inch short of six feet and who weighed two-thirty.

"Come in, Johnny."

Lowering his gaze, the saloonkeeper pretended to be concerned with a pile of invoices before him. Gaze still lowered, he indicated a straight-legged cushioned chair.

"Have a seat."

Johnny took the chair and said, "Got time to give me some advice, Mr. Veblen?"

"Call me Eric. You make me feel old."

Johnny kept waiting for him to push the papers aside and swivel the chair about. Veblen didn't.

"What's your trouble, Johnny?"

"Downstairs?"

"I heard that."

"I want to talk with you about Joe Hooker. About his ranch and—uh, *your* daughter, Treva."

"All right."

"As you know, I shot Joe Hooker, and he died on the way in. He told me about his land and buildings. About the feud he'd been having with Barlow Clesson and the Fiddleback. I got the idea Joe wanted me to move onto his ranch, get it to going again and turn it over to Treva. What do you think about it?"

Still concerned with the invoices, Veblen said, "Oh, I don't know. Be pretty hard to do."

"It was pretty hard to watch Joe die."

Veblen said, "I don't know how you're going to fit in, just yet." He looked around.

"What do you mean?"

"Treva will cause you a lot of trouble for nothing."

Johnny shook his head. "It won't be for nothing."

Veblen said, "There's something wrong out there. I don't know what, but no one could try harder than Joe tried. Treva could take all the money I have and move onto that place. Fight the Fiddleback. And she'd soon be as poverty-stricken there as her mother was."

Johnny hunted for a convincing argument, and said, "I'll stick with it."

"I don't doubt that you will. It's Treva I'm thinking of."

The saloonkeeper shoved the chair away from the desk. He swiveled to face Johnny. He leaned back and clasped his hands across the heavy gold watch chain which spanned his chest.

"Let's do a little figuring, Johnny. To make a real ranch out of that place, you'll need money for repairs, cow ponies, hiring hands, building fences, maybe. And you'll need at least two thousand head of she-stuff. And then it would be several years before you could hope to break even. The bank is hard to tap. Where are you expecting to get the money—from me?"

"Eric, I didn't come here for any of your money. If you were familiar with cattle brands in Wyoming Territory, you'd know I don't need to. My folks will lend me money, and I have a little of my own."

Veblen said, "I'm glad to hear that, Johnny. But your plans include Treva and her land, and she has ideas of her own. You just tangled with one of them."

"Downstairs?"

Veblen nodded. His jowled features hardened. "I don't intend to let him have her, though."

"Well, Eric, you can't keep her from marrying."

"I'm not trying to keep her from marrying. I wish she would. I'd like to see her marry Billy Phillips."

Johnny stared. "That preacher? Why, she wouldn't like that kind of life. Her hide's not thick enough. You got any idea what a preacher's wife has to put up with?"

"No."

Johnny shifted in the chair, wondering if he should forget Eric Veblen's preferences and do his palavering only with the girl.

Veblen said, "Did you know Minch Jayson?"

"No. Why do you ask?"

"Sizing you up. I figured you knew about him, and kept quiet."

Johnny shook his head. After a moment, he asked, "You don't care if I try to change Treva's mind, do you?"

"No. I wish you luck," Veblen told him. "You'll need every bit you can get."

Treva Veblen was riding through hot sunshine down the slope of a winding ridge, facing the rough flank of the mountain. She was wearing boots and jeans and a broad-brimmed hat, and bestrode a bay mare, forking a man's saddle with the stirrup leathers shortened. The rig was, of course, much too large for her. Her own kak was a sidesaddle, which was fine for a ride of short duration, Johnny McVay had told her, but if a girl kept her leg hooked around the curved horn of such a kak for a whole day, she had some black and blue marks to show for it—if she wanted to show it. Johnny knew what he was talking about, because back in Wyoming, a girl he had known had shown him.

Treva's new garb was wholly Johnny's idea, and he had accompanied her to the Emporium to buy it. She had been a little embarrassed after putting it on.

It was afternoon now, but this morning Treva and Johnny had ridden across stretches of shimmering prairie where wildflowers grew and butterflies flitted, where grasshoppers made their staccato rackets winging away from the horses and where preying hawks soared. Now and then she had passed thorny bushes of yellow plums growing in small, dense thickets.

The trail had forged between tangles of berry vines, sumac bushes, scattered boulders, foreign to these parts, and through head-high stands of weeds and stirrup-high grass. Where the grass was lush, Johnny McVay and Treva Veblen had stopped to graze their horses.

A lean old wolf, nose to the ground, had trotted in front of Treva, from one grass patch to another, and later the girl had reined in where a snake had crossed a playa of barren dust. She marveled aloud at the illusion created by the snake, saying she always found it impossible to understand how a snake could wiggle forward in zigzag fashion and leave a groove in the dust that was arrow-straight.

"Ever see a sidewinder?" Johnny asked.

"What is a sidewinder?"

"Sidewinders don't wiggle," Johnny told her. "They throw themselves."

When they were about ten miles from the precipice on the mountainside, Johnny pulled his gray to a stop. He cast a glance from right to left. Nearer on the right was the green fringe of woods along Big Goose Creek. Far to the left, unseen behind the hills, stood the headquarters layout of the Fiddleback ranch.

"From here to the barranca, the land is yours, Treva."

Beneath the hatbrim her features were intent as she gazed about, and Johnny could tell how she felt. This didn't seem like much for someone to have, after so many years of trouble to hold it.

Finally she said, "Eric thinks that Barlow Clesson might really have paid for this land, but Tom says he didn't. Tom says Eric would think that, anyway. Tom was with Joe more, and he ought to have a better idea of the straight of it. Wouldn't he?"

Johnny said, "This is all recorded in the county courthouse. You own this land, as I said. I was with Joe, too, when it mattered most of all. It doesn't make any difference what either Eric or Tom Saxon, thinks, if you stick with me."

Her expression brightened.

"Nothing in the world compares with ranch life," Johnny continued. "You'll love it."

Keeping an even distance from the flank of the mountain, Johnny led the girl down into a brushy draw. They saw trees ahead.

Johnny said, "That stand of timber marks a water-hole. We'd better stop there and rest."

Beyond the water-hole motte, a cleft in the barranca was visible. This, according to Johnny's uncle, was a box canyon.

The old Hooker ranch house, the house in which Treva had been born, stood on the alluvial fan to the right of this draw and on the bend of Big Goose Creek. A divide separated this Little Goose watershed from that of Big Goose, while this draw itself led straight to the canyon.

The water-hole motte consisted of sycamore and ash and elm, with a few pecan trees. Towering above all were gnarled old cottonwoods, which meant that the sycamores were just gaining a toehold here; ordinarily in these parts a scaly old sycamore was the tallest water-hole tree.

The water-hole was about an acre of marsh with no run-off. Where cattle hadn't trampled paths, it was fringed with willows. Heads up, half a dozen steers with oversloped earmarks and wide-twisting horns trotted down the draw. They stopped to look back at Treva and Johnny.

"Are those mine?" Treva asked.

"All Fiddleback. You haven't got any cattle yet," Johnny said. "I'm going to have to teach you to read brands and earmarks."

Johnny swung down from the saddle before the girl did, and immediately the steers became snuffy. They whirled away, bucking into lumbering runs, far more afraid of a man afoot than when he straddled a bronc.

While Treva quenched her thirst, bathed her face and shiny dark head, and moved about in the shade to get the saddle kinks out of her body, Johnny ground-tied his gray and watered the girl's mare. Then he tossed his hat aside, as Treva had done, and sat down near her with his back to a tree. He rolled and lit a smoke, and watched the way her dampened hair conformed to her pretty head. He thought then of Tom Saxon and frowned.

"Think you'll like having your own outfit, your own crew of riders?" Johnny asked.

She nodded. "When I get used to riding a horse."

After a moment Johnny said, "You understand about Joe Hooker, don't you?"

"Yes. No one really blames you, Johnny."

But Tom Saxon did, Johnny silently recalled.

Johnny said, "The Fiddleback has been using

your place, calling it a line camp. I'm going to take a walk up yonder to those blackjacks and see if any Fiddleback hands are there now, before we ride in on them. I don't know whether they would be hostile or not."

"If they are," Treva asked, "what'll we do?"

"Leave. But I'll guarantee you the next time you come, they won't be here."

Johnny McVay got up, went through the brush a short distance and angled up the slope; then walked west along the ridge to a stand of blackjacks. He went through them to the rim of the bluff. Tugging his hat lower against the westering sun, he became intent on the view below.

Since they had spoken of it as a line camp, he wasn't expecting much, but he saw a ranch house, bunkhouse, cookshack, barns, lean-to's, sheds, a wide expanse of corrals, and north toward Big Goose Creek was a three-cornered stretch of meadow that had been regularly mowed.

The ranch house was ell-shaped, built of hewn logs. Three chimneys of rock lifted above its roof shakes, and the shakes weren't more than two years old. Obviously the Fiddleback had kept the buildings in good repair.

The main house, although built low, cast a long shadow at this hour, and at the hitching bar Johnny saw a team and buckboard. The team was the only visible life about the place.

Near the sumac-choked mouth of the canyon, a bunch of cattle grazed but otherwise, save for brilliant-plumed birds flitting in the edge of the timber along the creek beyond the meadow, nothing moved.

Whoever had tied the team was inside the house and didn't intend to come out soon, Johnny decided, and he turned back through the blackjacks and descended into the draw where Treva sat in the shade.

"I saw a buckboard and team, but couldn't tell who's there. The corrals are empty. Sure looks good. You haven't been back out here since you left?"

Treva shook her head. "I didn't leave, Johnny. My mother took me away."

Johnny McVay helped her to her feet, considering her mighty pretty in blouse and jeans and boots, and put her into the saddle.

CHAPTER VI

A short ride brought them around in front of the bluff. The team and buckboard no longer stood in front of the ranch house, nor was it in sight on the trail to the Fiddleback headquarters. That road was visible for at least a mile as it followed along the base of the barranca.

A few minutes later when Johnny McVay and Treva Veblen rode around there, they found the team and buckboard hitched at the gallery that ran along the rear of the ell.

Connie Clesson was standing on the gallery, watching a man lift bedding, cooking utensils and other line-camp necessities, off the porch to pack in the buckboard. Johnny looked at the Fiddleback hand.

From hat to boots the man was straight and tall. He was wearing a fawn-colored vest and leather cuffs over a dark flannel shirt, and although Johnny saw no need for them, bullhide chaps. His spurs were nickel-plated. His black gun-harness showed well-oiled care. He was raven-haired, lean of face, and with a slightly flattened nose. He had shaved around a mustache, and his thin-lipped mouth had a hard look.

Preferring riding skirts, Connie Clesson had on one of brown denim today, and her shirt was of the same material, even though she had obviously arrived here on the seat of the buckboard where a housedress would have sufficed. Johnny McVay hadn't yet seen her looking entirely feminine, and he was speculating on it.

On the other hand, he knew what Treva would look like when she became a housewife.

Connie said, "With my father dead and yours, too, I've decided I won't quarrel over the house you were born in."

" 'Won't'?" Treva asked. "Or 'can't'?"

A worried frown appeared on Connie's brow.

As Johnny helped Treva down from the saddle and led her mare and his gray toward the corral fence, he heard Treva say, "How are you, Chris?"

"Fine. First time I ever saw you wearing pants."

"First time anyone's seen me."

"What will Tom say?"

"Oh, he'll throw a fit if he sees me."

"He's good at that, isn't he?"

Treva said, "Well—"

"I've been told you're dating the preacher now," Connie said. "What'll Tom say about that?"

"I'm not dating him. I've been with him a couple of times."

Chris Hogarth said, "Your idea or Eric's?"

"Eric's, of course, Chris."

Johnny McVay, having tied the horses and loosened their cinches, started toward the gallery.

Chris Hogarth, however, had no intention of being friendly. Cutting Johnny a dour look, the Fiddleback foreman stepped off the gallery and went toward the bunkhouse.

The two girls seated themselves on the edge of the gallery. Johnny pushed his hat back and hunkered on his spurs in front of the team.

Connie gave him a straight look. "I talked with Owen Tyndale. He said Treva holds title to ten sections here. Are we going to fight over the open range?"

Johnny inclined his head at Treva. "Ask her."

Connie looked at her.

Treva said, "Eric told me this place is worth ten thousand dollars or nothing. It's been worth nothing too long already. To anyone but the Fiddleback."

Connie said quickly, "I'll give you ten thousand for it."

Treva laughed. "You can't have it. You'll never get the house I was born in, Connie. Get that through your head."

Connie reddened. "Well, by gosh, we've already bought this place two or three times. Barlow paid for it at least twice, trying to deal with Joe Hooker. But that skunk—" She broke off and set her lips tight.

Treva said, "Barlow was worse than a skunk. He was a liar. He tried to ride roughshod over everyone. And did, too, until Oscar Rodin became sheriff. But now you Fiddlebackers watch your step in town, don't you?"

Johnny McVay lifted his chin with interest.

"Barlow had his faults," Connie said, "but telling lies about land and cattle wasn't one of them."

The team stamped and switched, jingling the harness. After a moment Johnny saw Hogarth returning, watching through the running gear of the buckboard. Now it was Johnny McVay who was in no mood to say howdy. He got up and stepped onto the gallery and entered the ranch house.

He stayed inside until he heard the buckboard rattling south on the Fiddleback road.

Coming out into the yard, he glanced at the departing rig, and went to all the buildings, looking in. Finding no one else about, he returned to Treva.

She was inspecting the rooms. Most of them were filled with furniture that Joe Hooker had ridden away from. None of it, except the cook-stove, had been here more than ten years, nor was it as expensive as that which he'd replaced.

Dreamy expression on her face, Treva stood at a bedroom closet, looking at a child's crib.

"Was that yours?" Johnny asked gently.

She came out of her reverie, looked around and laughed. "I don't know."

"A man handy with tools and a paintbrush

could make a mighty pretty little bed out of it."

"You do that, Johnny."

"Will you help me fill it?"

"Huh? Oh. No, I'm afraid not, Johnny," she told him, and shut the door.

Back in town, Johnny McVay slept with his door open and the windows raised. The roof of the hotel veranda sloped away from his front windows. On this morning the sun was an hour high when he awakened.

The first thing he became aware of was a splitting headache. In the Silver Saddle last night he had mixed whisky and beer, drinking with one man and then another, and now it seemed his head was swelling and shrinking rhythmically.

He got out of bed and closed the door and turned to the washstand and the pitcher of water. It was brackish, but it put some of the fire out inside him. He was pulling on his boots when he heard bootsteps in the hall. There were two pair, and they stopped at his door. Before there was time for a rap, Johnny called, "Shove on in."

Masefield and Creighton entered, and the grizzled man said, "You slept all day yesterday, didn't you? We were up three times; the last you were gone."

"Yeah," Johnny said. "Sit down." He had only two chairs. "Lay my gunbelt here on the bed, Pete."

Johnny was sitting on the bed. He stood up to settle his feet in his boots, and sank down again. He looked from one to the other.

Pete Creighton said, "Vern's made a deal for twenty head of mustangs."

"How much did you pay down on them?"

Masefield said, "A hundred dollars."

"Well," Johnny said, "I took Treva out there, and on the way back she told me something that's got me doubting. She liked my proposition just fine except for one thing. She told me Tom Saxon would shoot me if she moved out there with me. I said, 'I'm pretty good at that, myself.' That scared her. She asked me not to have any more trouble with him. Thinking of Joe, I guess."

The grizzled waddy said, "Well, what now, Johnny?"

"I told her what we were fixing to do, but she said she'd rather I waited. Said she might be able to work it out some way. I doubt it. She doesn't want me to hire any men or buy a remuda."

Masefield and Creighton exchanged a glance. Masefield said, "That lets us out, then, Pete."

"Maybe not."

"Keep the money you've got left," Johnny said. "That ought to square things."

"I'll know what I'm doing before I help buy any more horses," Creighton said.

"Johnny eased us over a tight spot. That's something," Masefield said. He looked at Johnny.

"Cade Brewster bought those horses for us. If you don't take them, he might not be able to turn them back."

Creighton said, "The man asked Vern sixty dollars, but he wanted cash right then, and you were gone. Brewster offered fifty-five and got them. Vern then paid Brewster a hundred dollars earnest money to hold them for you. At sixty."

"Tell Brewster to look for another buyer. If he finds one and gets sixty, I want my hundred back."

When Masefield and Creighton went out, pulling the door shut, Johnny belted on his Remington .44 and followed the sound of their spurred boots. He turned into the hotel dining room, however, to tank up on coffee.

Afterward, having left his mug and brush at the barbershop, he went up there for a shave, and was feeling almost normal again when he emerged. Squinting into the sunshine, he saw a familiar figure coming down the slope. He stood near the striped pole and waited.

The Reverend Billy Phillips came on and marched right past. Under his Mormon-style hat, his eyes were straight ahead.

Johnny said, "Brother Phillips."

The preacher marched on a few steps, but then stopped suddenly, turning about.

Blond features guarded, hat canted over a narrowed blue eye, Johnny McVay approached him. Johnny said, "Have I done something you disapprove of?"

"Yes, you have." The young preacher's face was grave. Standing pale and tense, the minister turned his attention to the public well. His face suddenly contorting, he whirled. "Why did you insist on her wearing britches? The women of this town are ladies."

"Well-uh, it was a long ways over there. Lots of brush and briers, and I figured a dress might become embarrassing."

After a moment Billy Phillips flushed and smiled.

Johnny continued, "I reckon I just didn't know how it was down here. Up in Wyoming all the women wear jeans. My mother wears them all the time when she's riding a horse."

"Different places have different customs," the preacher said. "Women didn't even ride astraddle in my home town, and it took me quite a while to become accustomed to divided skirts."

Johnny nodded. "We won't be doing any more riding together."

"Oh, it isn't that," the preacher said, but he didn't explain what it was. He and Johnny moved on to the corner, where Billy Phillips turned into the drugstore.

Johnny McVay stood on the corner, smoking a cigarette. His purpose was that of making himself conspicuous to the wide-shouldered man in the kipskin vest, the man with the ivory-handled six-shooter, standing at the well. Tom Saxon's snake-banded hat tilted far back on his tawny mane, Saxon was watching another man who had drawn himself a fresh drink.

That man was burly of frame, and his heavy jaws were stubbled with brown beard. Johnny noticed the thimble belt full of cartridges and the black-butted Colt. There was a tear in the fellow's hat that could have been made by a bullet.

They pitched their talk low, but Johnny heard the burly man say, "It's a deal, then, Tom. You can count on it."

Johnny had pistol-whipped Tom Saxon, and Saxon had taken backwater. Either he was a man you could trust, one to tie to, or he was capable of burying a grudge so deep that you'd be caught napping. Johnny was wary of any man who could suffer public humiliation with the poise that Saxon had displayed.

When Saxon caught sight of Johnny, he looked startled, but he picked up his talk with the burly man again as though he hadn't noticed Johnny McVay.

Johnny stepped off the boardwalk, cut across the dusty street to pass under the trees of the plaza, and headed for his uncle's office. But only Marshal Fenwick was there, standing at a south window, paring his nails with a bowie.

"Where's Uncle Oscar?"

"He's gone to see about his deputy."

"What's wrong with Wade?"

"Ain't been home in a couple of days. You going to be here now, Johnny? I've got some business of my own to tend to."

"Go ahead. How did you come out with Tyndale and Veblen?"

The marshal scraped an itching cheek with the bowie point. "They told me to wait. But if they get that reward and don't come across, I'll catch them with their tails in a crack sometime."

"Tyndale said he would make it right with you."

Marshal Fenwick grunted, started to leave. Then, as an afterthought: "Masefield and Creighton are looking for you. Said they'd wait outside. Go see what they want, Johnny. I told Oscar I'd stay here till he got back, and I'd better do it."

Outside on the stoop, Johnny paused to look around. Masefield and Creighton were hunkered in the shade of a tree.

Johnny kept standing, liking the roundabout noises. He heard wood chopping here and there, the ring of hammered metal, a distant clattering of a wagon, a horse racing along a side street, the barking of a far-off dog. He enjoyed the smells, too: dry dust and dust which carried the scent of water spilled at the well, ammonia from the stables, cooking odors, cigar smoke from a group of men in front of the bank.

Johnny McVay was beginning now to see himself as belonging here. He was fast becoming a part of the community, instead of just Sheriff Rodin's visiting nephew. Folks were beginning to look on him as an individual, Johnny McVay.

This Grief Hill, he decided, was a good town. A good place for a man to settle in—or near.

Moving on down the steps, Johnny hunkered down, and Masefield said to him, "There's a feed bill at the wagon yard against those horses."

"Let's go look at them," Johnny said, rising. "I may just pay for those cussed broncs and sell them to someone, myself. Or trade them."

Logan's freight layout, his wagon yard, office, blacksmith shop, stables and corrals, stood south of the Emporium. Johnny and the men with him climbed over the main gate into an area filled with Murphy wagons and orderly stacks and rows of parts. Some of the wagons were being repaired; others, greased. None of the workmen took notice of the three range-clad men. They climbed a second gate and went among barns and stables. Men with pitchforks were working in the stables, and the lot was filled with mules. Behind this second fenced area was a number of smaller corrals, most of them empty.

Climbing onto the fence of the corral Masefield and Creighton indicated, Johnny sat there running his gaze over the pen of mustangs. One blazed-face black caught his eye and made his pulse quicken. He was mistaken, though. The horse wasn't his.

On either side of him, Creighton and Masefield rolled smokes. Tightening the yellow drawstring of his tobacco sack with his teeth, the swarthy Creighton said, "They're all saddle broke, Johnny."

"Yonder comes Cade," Masefield said.

Johnny McVay glanced around and then he reversed his position on the top rail. Cade Brewster was the burly man whom Tom Saxon had been palavering with at the public well. Johnny got down off the fence and so did the other two.

"Cade," Masefield said, "Johnny's decided he'll take these broncs."

Cade Brewster was breathing heavily from a fast walk and the hurried climbing of two gates. He looked at Johnny. "You can't have them."

"Suits me."

Brewster swung his attention back to the grizzled man. "Did you mention that feed bill?"

Vern said, "I told him."

"How big is it?" Johnny asked.

"Five dollars a head."

"Twenty-two times five. A hundred and ten dollars."

"A hundred. Two of them broncs are my personal mounts."

Johnny mopped his face with his neckerchief.

"You've got the hundred that Vern gave you to bind the bargain."

"He told me to keep it, and find another buyer."

"Well," Johnny said, "I'll split the feed bill with you. How's that?"

Brewster moved his heavy jaws from side to side. "I ain't got no reason for giving you fifty dollars."

Johnny said, "Then let me pay the feed bill and give you a check for eleven hundred. You write me a bill of sale for twenty broncs."

Creighton rubbed his swarthy jaw. "Split the feed bill with him, Cade. You can afford to."

"And he can afford for me not to."

The grizzled Masefield said, "The way I look at it, Johnny—these horses did belong to you while they were eating up that feed bill. They belonged to you until we asked Cade to call the deal off."

Tight-lipped, Johnny moved his attention back to Brewster. "Write me out a bill of sale," he repeated.

"You can't have them, dang it!" Brewster's piglike eyes held a rabid glare, and his loud voice had carried to Logan's employees.

Expecting trouble, they began congregating in the adjoining corral to become innocent onlookers. The noise of labor throughout the yard had stilled.

If Vern Masefield hadn't essayed to use logic, Johnny would probably have argued further.

Now he took out a roll of bills and peeled off a hundred dollars. He stepped forward, offering the money to the burly man.

Brewster took it with a savage jerk, saying, "Better get it before you change your cussed mind."

Masefield and Creighton left the wagon yard with Brewster.

CHAPTER VII

Opposite the wagon yard stood five comfortable homes. Deputy Smollet, his wife Lucy and his young one, Mike, lived in the one on the north end, which Smollet owned. Sheriff Rodin had gone there to find out about Wade's absence. Johnny McVay angled that way now, having walked through Logan's gate ahead of a sixteen-mule jerkline outfit. The big Murphy wagon and trailer was heading south, deeper into Texas.

The Smollet yard was fenced. The front porch was verdant with morning-glory vines, completely enclosed except for the steps.

Letting himself through the gate and walking up the path, Johnny could see into the living room, where Mike, wearing only a diaper, was on his back on a pallet. Mike was playing with his toes, while Mrs. Smollet was stirring the air above him with a palm-leaf fan.

When Johnny stopped at the steps, taking his hat off, Lucy Smollet said, "Come on in, Johnny."

"No. Has Uncle Oscar already gone?"

Lucy was a buxom redhead, neat as a pin in a dress of pure white. Beneath the dress peeped moccasins. She stood up and came out on the porch, saying, "Why, he left a smart while ago."

Johnny nodded. "How are you getting along?"

"Fine as frog hair. Not wanting for anything. With Wade gone off on business, I don't even have to draw my own water or chop my own wood."

"Oh? Who does it?"

"Oscar. Or he sends some other feller to do it. Steve came once. Bedford Polk drawed my last wash water."

Johnny lowered his gaze to the living room floor. He grinned. "Mike seems to be doing all right."

"Yes, but he's spoiled rotten. I had him asleep, but Oscar made me wake him up so he could romp with him. I feel so sorry for Oscar sometimes."

"You mean about his family?"

Lucy nodded and cut a glance at the fan. Long ago, while Rodin was off on Ranger duty, the Comanches had massacred his family—just for spite, he had told Lucy.

"Well," Johnny said, "I reckon I'd better be going."

"Can't spend all your money in one place, eh?"

Johnny gestured at the wagon yard. "I just spent a hundred dollars over there."

He walked on past the vacant lot, entered the restaurant and ate a late breakfast and returned to the courthouse.

Sheriff Rodin was standing in his doorway. He turned back for Johnny to follow him into the office. Seated, he said, "I was fixing to send somebody after you."

"What did you want?"

"You take a ride down Little Goose Creek and see what's keeping Wade."

Johnny straddled a chair. "Wade thought Sammy Lee would sneak back home sooner or later. He intended to hide out there and keep watch."

"That's what I told him to do, but he should of been home before now. I didn't aim for him to stay down there day and night."

"Barlow's money is stashed there," Johnny said. "Or was."

Rodin's gaunt, chin-whiskered face was gloomy. "I'm hoping not to worry about that—deciding if it's Connie's, or if Eric ought to get it back."

"To settle the argument," Johnny said, "let me have it."

"There you go now. This ain't no time for funning." Rodin gestured with a forefinger. "Want me to deputize you?"

"No," Johnny said. He got up and went to the gun rack, taking down his carbine. "Tom Saxon might think I was hiding behind it." He paused. "Why not ask those nesters on the plaza about Wade? Might save a long ride."

"Johnny, if you'll stay here in the office—"

"I'm going, Uncle Oscar. Can't leave right away, though."

"Uh-huh. Steve said you pistol-whipped Tom because he called you a kid."

"Who is Tom Saxon?" Johnny countered.

"That's who he is. Comes from a fine family in Austin. I knowed his folks, all of them. He's a right fine feller, Tom is."

Johnny pushed back his hat. "I didn't tangle with him because he called me a kid. He grabbed my clothes and jerked me around. Scared me by making a face at me."

"Uh-huh. Well, he's dangerous, Johnny. Don't reckon he aims to push it, though, or he'd of been all over you by now."

Johnny left the courthouse frowning.

He met Pablo Cardoza on the plaza. "Feed my gray this morning?"

"Of course, Juanito."

"Want to saddle him and tie him in front of the saloon?"

"*Si.*"

Handing Pablo the carbine, Johnny cut back toward the saloon, feeling great need for a remedial hair of the dog.

Pushing through the swinging doors, he glanced along the line of men at the bar. He knew none. The gambling layouts, except for one big green-covered poker table, were not running. The men playing poker and those at the tables with bottles and glasses before them were also unknown to Johnny. Walking deeper into the room, he called for whisky.

The bartender drew a dram of bust-head from the spigot.

Johnny drank it neat and called for another, one to sip slowly, to savor, to sustain him during the ride ahead.

Over at the piano the frock-coated old perfessor was expertly rendering high-faluting, brought-on foreign stuff. Johnny thought of asking him to play The Girl I Left Behind Me, but decided not to. Man might not even know it.

Johnny finished the second dram and considered having a third, but at this moment the piano music ended with an expertly produced crash.

The sudden hush was broken by little sounds—boots scuffing the sawdust, a spur tinkle, a deck being riffled, clink and thud of bottle and glass, low-pitched voices.

Suddenly from the mezzanine, came a shout of anger. There was the racketing crash of a cowhand falling downstairs, and Johnny McVay stepped away from the bar for a better look.

The falling man was Tom Saxon. Halfway downstairs he grabbed the bannister, got his boots back under him and came erect.

Hair tousled, coat collar awry, the saloonkeeper was watching him from the mezzanine, his jowled visage dark with anger.

Saxon slapped a hand to his holster and found it empty. He glanced down and saw the ivory-handled weapon on the tread above him. He scooped it up and thumbed back the hammer, his features twisting savagely. The saloonkeeper stood motionless. Those in the room saw shock in his face. Eric Veblen expected to die.

His tawny hair swinging across his flushed brow, Saxon kept his finger on the trigger. He said, "I'll put it away and we'll start even."

Johnny McVay thought, He's afraid to, or he'd have done it without saying anything.

Veblen watched him.

"Aren't you packing a gun?"

The saloonkeeper only stared, but now the color was gone from his face.

With a supple-fingered gesture, Saxon let the hammer down and hurled the six-shooter upward. Veblen caught it.

"Shoot," Saxon said, "because I'm coming up there and beat your guts out!"

Veblen gave the gun a flip. He grasped it by the barrel and held it out.

Shoulders slumping, chin dropping, Saxon climbed the stairs. He didn't reach for the gun, but no one expected him to. He walked past Veblen, and both men disappeared into the office.

The noise in the saloon surged up loud. One of

the men at the bar said, "If Saxon had knowed about Minch—"

"He did," another said. "He was here that morning."

Johnny McVay was sober of mien when he went out through the batwings. He knew one thing for sure now. He couldn't afford to have more trouble with Tom Saxon, even if he had to dodge Tom. The man from Austin just wasn't up to his class, and Johnny wanted Saxon to keep his self-respect.

Pablo Cardoza had tied the gray at the Silver Saddle hitch rail. While Johnny was tightening the cinches, he heard a distant rataplan of many hoofbeats coming from the north. The racing hoofs thundered on the heavy bridge timbers. When they hit the main street, the cavalcade checked their mounts abruptly. As the dust cleared, Johnny saw Connie Clesson and part of her Fiddleback crew.

Generally the Fiddlebackers stopped first at the hotel, where Connie would dismount and one of her hands would lead her pony on to the livery stable. Today she came on with her men, with Hogarth and Maisie flanking her. The only other man Johnny knew was McVickers.

Johnny was tying his latigo when the cavalcade drew even with him. They stopped their horses. Looking at Connie's pretty face, Johnny McVay touched his hatbrim.

She said, "Moved any cattle out there yet?"

"No."

Chris Hogarth was glint-eyed and scowling, his high-boned and flat-nosed visage filling Johnny with sudden fury. Johnny shifted his attention to Clete Maisie, though, and back to Connie.

"I've about gotten over my father's death," she said, her jaw thrust forward, "and I'm beginning to think straight again. I consider that place part of the Fiddleback, and you'll lose everything you put there."

"Well, Treva didn't seem too interested."

"What?"

"She didn't ask *me* to tangle with you."

Flushing, Connie said, "Well, you can pull out, can't you?" She took her men on down the street.

The northbound stagecoach passed Johnny McVay as he rode toward Little Goose Creek. Beyond the crossing, he reined on to the north fork and jogged along in the sunshine at the edge of the timber, jay birds racketing throughout the bosque and field larks warbling on the prairie to the left. Far off, the westering sun laid a haze over the ravines and canyons and made the mountain a solid-looking wall.

Approaching Sammy Lee Dilts's place, Johnny watched a hawk fan its tail as it braked its flight to perch on the topmost branch of the lone tree out on the prairie. He was thinking what a fool

Sammy Lee was, getting mixed up in a robbing and killing when he had such country as this to live in, to work with, to gaze at and enjoy; and when he had a girl such as Rebecca Casper eager to share it with him.

Rounding a point of the bosque, Johnny had a view of Dilts's house. He squinted thoughtfully. A wagon and team was backed up to the porch. It was Sammy Lee's wagon, but a man and boy were loading furniture into it. Johnny had seen them before, passing this place. A woman had been with them then. They were alone now.

The boy was on the porch; the man was in the wagon, placing a knocked-down bedstead among the load.

Riding into the yard, Johnny said, "Who told you to take this stuff, mister?"

The man was broad of face and mustached. He was sweating profusely, his hickory shirt and baggy cotton trousers plastered to his heavyset body. Johnny noticed his wide galluses; salt and sweat had grimed his slouch hat.

"It's mine. I bought Sammy Lee out. Want to see my bill of sale?"

"I sure do."

The man passed over a folded paper. Checking his fidgiting horse, Johnny perused the paper. Sammy Lee Dilts had signed it, and so had two witnesses, Virgil and Effie Casper.

Johnny handed the instrument back. "Where's Sammy Lee now, Mr. Delbert?"

Saul Delbert said, "Couldn't say. I dealt with him at the Caspers. Bought his crop and livestock and implements, besides this-here stuff. It's all down there in writing, ain't it?"

"You're within your rights. Have you seen Deputy Smollet lately?"

Walking back onto the porch, Saul Delbert turned and shook his head. "Not for quite a spell. You haven't, either, have you, Freddie?"

The towheaded, overalled kid said, "Naw."

Johnny McVay dismounted and tied his horse to the porch. He rolled and lit a cigarette.

Saul Delbert said, "This is our last load, and I'm purely glad it is. I could have bought this farm, too, dirt cheap, but I'm hoping they'll get that-there Clesson matter cleared up, and Sammy Lee'll come back."

"Did Sammy Lee say where he was going?"

"Up to The Nations. Virgil Casper can tell you more than I can. His gal Rebecca went, too."

Johnny slowly nodded. Wade Smollet had taken the trail, of course, but Johnny couldn't savvy why Wade hadn't first reported back to the sheriff. Still, he might have been so close he'd kept on, expecting every moment to collar Sammy Lee. He could cover mile after mile that way.

Stepping up on the porch, Johnny went along

the breezeway, glancing into the empty rooms. He continued on to the back porch, observing that Delbert had loaded the cedar bucket, basin and dipper. He had taken the rope and pulley and well bucket. Most men wouldn't have done that, depriving passers-by of a chance to drink. Delbert had bought it, though.

The horses, the cow and calf were gone from the barnlot. The chicken run and the hogpen were empty and the corncrib cleaned out.

Sammy Lee was guilty, Johnny told himself. He didn't ever intend to return.

Rounding the corner of the lot and continuing along the path, Johnny went down the steep creek bank to the first bottom. The jackstraw pile of logs was there, but the tools were gone. The big cast iron kettle had been taken. For a while, Johnny studied the spot where it had sat. He picked up a stick and thrust it into the ground, and then he knew.

Barlow Clesson's poker winnings had been hidden beneath the kettle. The ashes had been raked aside, the money dug up, and the ashes replaced. Sammy Lee had headed for The Nations well heeled.

Johnny went back up to the house.

Saul Delbert and the boy were on the spring seat ready to pull the load away.

"Mr. Delbert, did you do any digging under the wash kettle?"

Expression blank, Saul Delbert's broad, mustached face moved from side to side. "No, I didn't. You didn't, either, did you, Freddie?"

"Naw. 'Course not."

Johnny McVay nodded. "That's all I wanted to know," he said, and the Delberts drove off with their load of furniture.

CHAPTER VIII

Astride his gray, Johnny McVay rode through the bosque, cutting for sign of Dilts and the deputy. He worked along both banks of the creek, and found nothing. An hour later, he put the horse along the road taken by the Delberts, riding between fields of tall corn dotted here and there with fire-blackened snags. The mountain to the west was silhouetted by a setting sun.

Johnny stopped at two nester places and asked about the deputy, but Wade Smollet hadn't been seen.

The third house he came to sat back on a knoll a hundred yards from the road and hemmed in by cornfields on both sides. The large frame house was square shaped and weathered. The trees around it on the elevation had been whitewashed. A smokehouse loomed directly behind it. Farther back were farm buildings.

The house had a tall rock chimney, but the smoke that rose from among the trees came from the kitchen stovepipe. The odors of fried meat and freshly baked bread greeted Johnny McVay when he reined off the main road.

This was the Casper place, he'd been told.

Johnny kept an eye out for the brown-and-white mongrel, but there was no sign of the dog.

Virgil Casper was a man the years had touched lightly. Of medium height and muscular build, he had a shock of brown hair and a smooth nut-brown countenance. Bareheaded, sleeves rolled high on his arms, he came out on the porch, thumbs hooked in the galluses of his blue bib overalls.

Johnny McVay had seen the Caspers in town, at a distance. Rebecca was the only one he had talked to. The girl's father now seemed apprehensive.

Reining in near the porch, Johnny said, "Are you Casper?"

The sodbuster nodded.

"How's the chance for supper and a feed for my horse? I'm Oscar Rodin's nephew."

"You're Johnny McVay, then. Light down." Casper came off the porch as Johnny dismounted and called back through the house, "Effie, fix an extra place. We've got company."

Feminine footsteps sounded, and Effie Casper came into view. She was complexioned like her husband and wore her black hair parted in the center, brushed back and gathered behind her head. She was a bright-eyed, small woman, neatly attired in a calico dress and kitchen apron.

"Are you here on official business, Mr. McVay?"

Johnny took off his Stetson. "I'm not a deputy sheriff, if that's what you mean."

"Rebecca said your Uncle Oscar wanted Sammy Lee to come to town. We couldn't get him to. Said they wasn't any use of making a goat out of him." Her tone was one of disapproval.

Johnny said, "I think Uncle Oscar mentioned something about getting Sammy Lee to help him look for Barlow Clesson's money."

"A body's just wasting time, looking to Sammy Lee for favors. All he's good at is sneaking around."

"Effie," her husband said sternly, "that's no way to talk!"

"Well, Virgil, I can't help it." Looking at Johnny again, she said, "Sammy Lee never did bring your horse back, did he?"

"No, ma'am."

"Sammy Lee left money with me to pay for the horse and saddle and rifle," Casper volunteered. "He wasn't trying to steal."

"Money he got from Saul Delbert?" Johnny asked.

"Yes, from Saul."

"Saul showed me a bill of sale. When did Sammy Lee sign that?"

"Right early yesterday morning."

"Did Sammy Lee have saddlebags?"

Casper nodded.

"Well," Johnny said, "we'll talk about it later." He turned to Mrs. Casper. "I'd like to stay all night if I won't be imposing."

"You won't be. I've been wishing all afternoon somebody would drop by. With Rebecca gone off up yonder to the Indian country, it seems so lonesome around here I can't hardly stand it." She glanced at her husband and said crisply, "You two go wash up. Supper's ready to put on the table."

Johnny led his horse and followed Casper around the house. "When did Sammy Lee and Rebecca leave?"

"Yesterday morning, while Saul was here."

There was water in the lot where Casper's horses and cows ran together. Casper emptied a measure of shelled corn into the box in one of the stalls, shook down a manger full of hay, and tied Johnny's gray there.

Returning to the back porch, they washed their hands and faces and combed their hair. The table was laden with food, and they ate supper leisurely, finishing the meal by lamplight.

With the table cleared and the dishes washed, Mrs. Casper removed her apron. Because of the thickly swarming insects, she blew out the lamp. Bright moonlight lay outside. Dragging chairs out onto the front porch, the three sat down to enjoy the comparative cool of the evening.

Casper filled his pipe. Johnny rolled a cigarette. Mrs. Casper rocked slowly in a chair that softly squeaked.

Below the whitewashed trees of the knoll, the

dusty road, the field beyond it, the Little Goose Creek bosque and the rolling hills in the distance were sharply etched in the moonlight. Farther down the creek, some sodbuster's dogs had treed a varmint, and one old hound had a hoarse bawl that carried for miles.

Tossing his cigarette into the yard, Johnny asked, "Did you have any other children?"

Mrs. Casper's chair stopped squeaking. "Two," she said. "Both died when they was babies." Her tone was forlorn.

"Rebecca's mighty pretty," Johnny said. "Me, I don't think I'd want a daughter of mine to go so far from home. You folks sure have a lot of confidence in Sammy Lee. Do you know much about him?"

Casper said, "He's a hard worker."

"Saul Delbert raised him," Mrs. Casper said. "The Diltses and the Delberts was neighbors up in Kansas. Sammy Lee's pa treated him so mean Saul took him in. When they loaded up and came down here, the Delberts brought Sammy Lee with them. He's had a right smart of schooling."

Casper said, "Sammy Lee's raising a fine crop of corn this year. He'll be a good provider, and that's what you have to think of first."

Johnny McVay shifted his Remington to a more comfortable position. "Did it ever occur to you that Sammy Lee is really running from the law?"

"Oh, no, he ain't running from the law," Casper said quickly. "He left on account of Chris Hogarth and Clete Maisie. Being there with them fellers who killed Barlow Clesson, Sammy Lee said, was just the same as signing his own death warrant. He said them Fiddleback men hated us farmers anyhow, and all they needed was an excuse."

"Yes," Johnny said. "Guess that's true enough."

Mrs. Casper said, "Do you think Rebecca would have been safe with Sammy Lee there on his place?"

"No," Johnny said.

The evening wore on.

The hounds had quit baying now, but from up the creek came the cacophony of screeches and squawks and hoots of a treeful of owls.

Johnny said, "I've heard our old cook, Shoo-fly Flynn, use the expression 'wise as a treeful of owls.' If there's anything more stupid than a treeful of owls on a moonlight night, I don't know what it is."

"Yes," Casper agreed, and after a time, Effie said, "When you're ready to go to bed, Mr. McVay, I'll show you to your room."

"My room is under one of those trees yonder. Be cooler. And if I decide to ride on during the night, I won't disturb you."

"Oh, you wouldn't disturb us," Mrs. Casper said, "but it'll be tolerable cooler."

When Johnny McVay stood up, Casper said, "If you do ride on, we sure have enjoyed your visit. Get him a blanket, Effie."

Johnny walked from the porch and spread the blanket atop a low bluff. He removed his gunbelt, boots and hat, and tucked the boots under the edge of the blanket for a pillow. He intended to sleep with one eye open, as the saying went, but he dropped off into a sound slumber.

Around midnight, the stagecoach bound for Grief Hill passed with a thunder of hoofs and a grinding of wheels, its running lights winking through the trees, the smell of dust lingering long in its wake. Silence reigned afterward, and Johnny went back to sleep.

Day was just breaking when he again opened his eyes. When he noticed the brown-and-white mongrel squatted a few feet from his blanket, he came instantly wide awake and sat up.

Silky ears swaying, the dog thumped its tail on the ground.

Keeping a close watch on the house, Johnny put on his hat and pulled on his boots. Alert, he stood erect to buckle on his gun harness. Gathering up the blanket, he folded it and carried it to the porch, watching and listening.

He didn't think that Sammy Lee's dog had returned alone. It didn't seem reasonable, either, that Sammy Lee, arriving during the night, would have gone to bed in the house when the sheriff's nephew was asleep under the trees. He would have been more inclined to put a slug through Johnny's head.

The Caspers wouldn't have warned Johnny about Sammy Lee. You couldn't expect them to, with Sammy Lee either a son-in-law or a prospective one.

The dog climbed up on the porch and lay down.

Hearing no sound from within, Johnny turned along the north side of the house. When he came to the end of the back porch, he again stopped to listen.

In the brightening daylight he went around the smokehouse. On the fence near the lot gate were a saddle, blanket and bridle. It was Johnny's own gear, that which Sammy Lee had taken. Johnny then noticed among the horses in the lot his own blazed-face black gelding.

Hungry chickens came flocking from every direction when he let himself into the barnlot. The penned-up calves began to blat. Making a familiar noise with his lips, Johnny went among the horses. He walked up to his gelding and patted the bronc on the neck. He walked around him, looking for cuts or bruises. There were none. Except for being gaunted, the gelding was in fine condition. Always able to make sixty miles in a day, he appeared to have traveled at least that far recently.

The lot gate rattled on its hinges, and Virgil

Casper, appeared, looking as though he had just gotten out of bed. His brown shock of hair was still sleep tangled. He came between a couple of cows to reach Johnny, and commingled emotions contorted his smooth brown features.

Johnny said, "Rebecca came home during the night, didn't she, Virgil?"

"She purely did."

"I must have been sleeping like a log."

"Why, I thought you was awake. You told the dog to get out. Spot was licking your face."

"I don't remember it," Johnny said, and then he asked, "Did Deputy Smollet collar Sammy Lee?"

"The deputy's dead."

Johnny stared.

Casper licked his lips. Face sorely troubled, he said, "I wish to heaven I could read people. Sammy Lee's a killer. He shot Deputy Smollet dead."

Johnny McVay stood there a moment with downcast eyes. He was thinking of Lucy's losing a husband and of Mike's losing a father. Looking up, he asked, "Where did it happen?"

Casper said, "On the mountain, way the yonder side of Big Goose Creek." He was gesturing toward the northwest at the high plains country.

"That's not the way to The Nations."

"I know it. Sammy Lee got afraid to pass them stage relay stations. He said they had telegraphs, and told Rebecca that Deputy Smollet would get

Wells-Fargo to stop him. Said they had better head for New Mexico."

"Sammy Lee bushwhacked Wade?"

Casper nodded. "Made Rebecca take the horses and go on, so there would be a trail for Mr. Smollet to follow. He told her they would leave him afoot. She heard a shot. She tied up Sammy Lee's horse— your gelding—and went back careful-like, not knowing if Sammy Lee had been hit. But he'd knocked Mr. Smollet out of the saddle. Sammy Lee told her to go get his horse. She knowed she aimed to make a run for it, and swapped. Got your gelding. Sammy Lee shot at her."

"Glad he didn't hit her," Johnny muttered. He asked then, "Have you got the saddlebags?"

"Yes, but the money wasn't in them. Sammy Lee had rolled it in Rebecca's tarp, to carry for him. She left it on her saddle, clothes and all."

Johnny said, "It doesn't matter." He stroked the gelding's mane, brows knitted. "I'll have to bring Wade's body back. I doubt that I could follow a map. Wonder if she will take me to him? You'd have to go, too, of course."

Casper scratched his head again. "We was expecting to, Mr. McVay. Effie can stay with her brother's folks, and he can come and do my chores. Be all right to let Rebecca finish her nap?"

"Why, of course," Johnny said quickly.

Combing fingers through his tousled hair, Casper became aware of the roundabout noise. "I'd better get my feeding and milking done."

"I'll help you."

"All right, Mr. McVay. If you want to, you can pump the trough full."

Although there was a pump in the barnlot, the well at the end of the porch had a rope and pulley. The pulley needed greasing. Hearing someone drawing a bucket of water, Johnny walked around to where he could see past the smokehouse.

It was Rebecca, but she wasn't looking at him.

The blazed-face gelding followed Johnny and gave him a reason for remaining within sight of the girl. He watched her wash her hands and face, douse her curly brown head, and bury her face in a fluffy towel. He kept his eyes on her intently as she headed for the kitchen. She was all right, he told himself. The supple, graceful way she walked revealed that she wasn't sore or stiff. Another long ride wouldn't be an imposition.

Johnny McVay couldn't milk, but he minded the calves, letting them suck until the cows started giving down, and then holding them off until Virgil had filled his bucket.

"Virgil," Mrs. Casper called, "are you men about ready for breakfast?"

"Just about, Effie."

When the two men finally entered the kitchen, Effie was at the stove and Rebecca was at the table filling the coffee cups from a gallon pot. She kept her curly head lowered.

"Rebecca," Johnny said, "don't blame yourself for Wade Smollet's death."

She looked up. "I didn't have any business being so silly. I should have known Sammy Lee was fixing to do something besides set that deputy afoot."

"You sure kept a cool head," Johnny told her, "and I appreciate your bringing back my gelding."

"I told you you'd get it."

"You told me something else. Do you expect me to do that now?"

A wry smile touched her lips. "Go home and stay there? That was silly, too. This valley needs gunfighters worse than Wyoming does."

Mrs. Casper walked over to them and gestured. "Let's eat. Mr. McVay, you take the same place."

Effie had spread her best tablecloth this morning, and had centered it with two big platters, one stacked with nicely browned fried ham, the other containing eggs cooked in the same skillet. There was a bowl of ham gravy, colored and flavored with a dash of coffee. There was a big mold of yellow butter, a tall pitcher of milk. Effie warned them that the milk tasted blinked to her. It was hard to keep it sweet overnight in weather like this, and Virgil hadn't ever gotten around to digging her a milk cellar. Nobody used milk still warm from the heat of the cow. Effie served the biscuits out of the baking pan, forcing them on Johnny McVay and her husband and daughter two at a time. She seemed to be getting up and down every minute or two, while Rebecca kept the coffee cups filled.

"Can we reach that place with a buckboard?" Johnny asked.

"We couldn't even get close," Rebecca told him. "It's almost too rough for horses."

Breakfast was over and Johnny walked out on the back porch to smoke a cigarette.

Rebecca came out of the kitchen with a plate of left-overs and went down into the yard. When her spoon made a scraping noise, the brown-and-white mongrel trotted out of the nearby cornfield.

Turning to Johnny McVay, the girl said, "Spot will always remind me of him."

"Spot quit Sammy Lee before you did, didn't he?"

"Yes. Maybe he's got more sense than I have."

Johnny smiled. "I always say the wrong thing."

"Well, that's not as bad as *doing* the wrong thing."

"You came home pretty fast. How did Spot keep up with my gelding?"

"I carried him across the saddle."

After a moment, Johnny said, "At a time like

that, Rebecca, with Sammy Lee shooting at me, I doubt if I would have stopped for a dog."

"Oh, I didn't stop for him till I was plumb away from Sammy Lee. Spot had a choice, and he followed me."

Hearing Virgil and Effie come out onto the porch, Johnny turned. Virgil said, "Get busy sacking up our grub, Effie, and don't forget salt and grease." He turned to Johnny. "A pound of coffee be enough?"

Johnny saw what Virgil was thinking. "We won't be gone long."

"Don't you want me to help you catch Sammy Lee?" Casper asked.

"That's a job for the law, Virgil. I'm not a deputy."

"Well, I ain't, either," Casper said, and looked relieved. "Just put in a skillet and that little coffeepot of your'n, Effie."

Going into the barnlot, Johnny and Virgil caught up Johnny's gray, a sorrel gelding and a roan mare. Saddling the gray, Johnny then cinched his new kak on the mare for Rebecca.

He asked Casper, "Got a sawbuck?"

The sodbuster nodded. "That brown pony yonder," Casper said, pointing, "is the best little pack animal in this whole country. It might not look it, but it'll tote Mr. Smollet easy enough. I'll get a wagon sheet."

Leading out of the lot, they tethered the saddle

horses to the fence and took the pony to the porch, where Effie had piled the sacks of grub, cooking utensils and blankets.

Rebecca had pulled a pair of overalls on over her dress and was wearing a poke bonnet.

Casper had no saddle gun, but he possessed a smallbore rifle and a .50 buffalo gun.

Johnny said, "You won't be shooting anything but a squirrel or quail, maybe."

"Might get a deer."

"I'll lend you my forty-four for that."

Casper looked thoughtful. "Well," he said, "then I reckon we're ready. Don't you worry now, Effie. We won't be gone a minute longer than we have to."

Mrs. Casper folded her arms. "I'll look for you when I see you coming. You or Rebecca, one, had better lock Spot in the crib, though, unless you aim to take him with you."

The three kept to the stage road and twice forded Little Goose Creek. When they had put their horses through the wide, shallow crossing of Big Goose Creek, they rode northwest through the brushy bottoms. Climbing to higher ground, they began threading among grass-covered hills. Finally they found themselves on the brink of a ravine, one wider and deeper than that which skirted the county seat.

Johnny said, "Rebecca, you didn't come this way?"

"No. I was trying to follow a beeline back to where Mr. Smollet is."

They rode along the brink of the *quebrada* for a mile before finding a place to cross it. Safely on the far side, Johnny said to the girl's father, "She was sure right about the buckboard."

"Oh, you could take one up there easily enough," Rebecca said. "One piece at a time."

CHAPTER IX

In the late evening they rode down into a hollow that contained a motte of tall trees and a hole of drinkable water. The trees were casting long, lean shadows by the time they got their horses unsaddled, watered and staked out. Walking back to the sandy spot where they had put their riding gear, packsaddle and camping gear, Virgil shouldered a windfall limb for firewood. While he and Johnny were breaking the limb into small chunks, Rebecca untied the sacks. She got out skillet and coffeepot.

Casper, eyes squinted thoughtfully, looked from Rebecca to Johnny McVay. He then lifted his glance toward the north end of the hollow, where a winding line of brush followed a watercourse down from the prairie.

"Mr. McVay, right about now if a man was laying low up yonder by that game trail he might kill a fat buck. Let me take your Henry rifle and mosey off up there."

"Help yourself."

Rebecca was on her knees in the sand. "Want me to fry some of this meat, Pa, or wait."

"Wait."

"Any danger from Indians?" Johnny asked.

"Not hereabouts. Would be if we was closer

to the Panhandle. Oklahoma Indians raid south of the Red every now and then, but they've quit depredating through these parts." Pushing back from the carefully laid pile of wood, he said, "No need to light it till you're ready to use it, Rebecca, as hot as it is."

"Go ahead and light it, Pa. I can wait for something to eat, but I want coffee right now."

With the blaze making the wood pop and crack, Casper got to his feet and brushed his hands. "Well, I'll go get that buck," he said, and with Johnny's carbine in the crook of his arm, he strode rapidly toward the line of brush.

The water hole was margined with hard sand and clumps of willows.

"Want me to fill the coffeepot?" Johnny asked.

Rebecca said, "You clean this skillet. It hasn't been used since goodness knows when, and it's rusty. Get a handful of wet sand and see how bright you can make it. Then I'll cure it."

"How?"

"Put some grease in it and get it smoking hot. You pour that grease out, because it's dirty. Has someone always done your cooking for you, Mr. McVay?"

"Not always. Cooking venison, I'd cut one of those green willows, put the meat on it and stick it in the ground so it would hang over the fire."

"But you'd rather have me fry it, hadn't you?"

"I'll eat it any way you fix it," Johnny said.

While Johnny was scouring the skillet, Rebecca came over and hunkered down beside him to fill the coffeepot. When he met her eyes, he found a feminine gleam in them.

"Sammy Lee ever kiss you?"

"No."

"And you planning to marry him? I don't believe it."

"Believe what you want to," she said, and presently asked, "Did you ever kiss a girl?"

"Lots of them."

"Well, Mr. McVay, here's one you won't kiss."

There was amusement in Rebecca's eyes as well as a challenge.

Johnny put the frying pan down, dipped his hands into the water to remove the sand, and then he caught her by an arm, pulling her towards him. He bent to kiss her.

She said, "Don't," and turned her face.

Johnny didn't release her. He reached to bring her averted face toward his. Suddenly she surged against him, pushing him backward, and then jerked free. At the same time, she brought the coffeepot around, water and all, and smacked him on the chin with it. The water sloshed over his vest and shirt as well as wetting the underside of his hat.

"Ah, what's the matter with you?" he said, and got to his feet.

"What's the matter with *you?*" Rebecca said.

She washed the pot, moved to clear water and refilled it, and carried it to the fire.

Sanding out the final speck of rust, Johnny was thinking what a fine girl Rebecca was. She deserved a good husband—a good sodbuster, like herself—not some poor devil of a hard-working, generally woman-starved cowhand.

A gunshot sounded up on the prairie after Johnny had taken her the skillet. He said, "That was my carbine," and he and Rebecca kept watching.

It wasn't long then until Casper appeared on the rim. He was empty-handed, however, and still quite a distance from camp, he shouted, "Fry that side-meat, Rebecca. I missed."

"Pa couldn't hit the ground with his hat," the girl said, and got busy preparing a meal.

When he reached camp, Casper looked Johnny McVay over. Expression wry, he asked, "Did you fall in?"

"Rebecca pushed me."

The girl said, "Johnny's the biggest liar you ever seen, Pa. I didn't touch him."

Casper's expression eased. He winked and said, "If she's anything like her ma is, Johnny, she gets a man to talk just so's she can call him a liar."

Darkness was closing in on the hollow by the time they had eaten their bread and meat and raw onions and had emptied the coffeepot. The air was so sultry that even heat from the glowing embers was uncomfortable. Rebecca drowned them. Her father and Johnny McVay went to bring the staked-out horses closer to camp. Casper then spread the wagon sheet for his daughter to put her blanket on. He and Johnny spread theirs on the smooth sand.

After a while, looking up at the stars, twinkling in a cloudless sky, Johnny thought of Lucy Smollet and her young one. He wondered how Lucy would bear up under her bereavement. Carrying Wade's body back was one chore he wished mightily he didn't have. . . .

They were in their saddles again by full daylight.

Near mid-morning they reached a sheep camp, where Johnny asked about Sammy Lee Dilts, thinking Dilts might have doubled back on his trail and stopped here for chuck. Sammy Lee hadn't.

"He's on his way to New Mexico, like I told you," the girl said.

"Might have changed his destination again on account of your knowing that," Johnny said, and the girl's father agreed.

They rode on.

The buffalo herds were farther north at this dry season, but nevertheless impotent old bulls were visible here and there. Wolves would get them. Casper declared it was a shame what Mother

Nature did about such matters, but they were too stringy and tough for human consumption.

Antelope were plentiful. One of these would have provided succulent steaks, but Casper begrudged the time it would have taken to kill one. They espied but one other horseback rider. He was far off and kept away from them. He was, Johnny finally made out, an Army mail courier.

Noon found Johnny McVay and the Caspers at the foot of the mountain. After refreshing themselves at a spring, they put their horses up among boulders, through stands of blackjacks, working from shelf to shelf, dodging bluffs and slopes too steep to climb.

Johnny McVay maintained that only in Texas would this elevation have been called a mountain, but when they had gained the summit, they and their horses exhausted, he was ready to concede that it was indeed a mountain. Widespreading oak trees in an open forest covered the flat mountain top. In mottled shade and sunshine under an oak, the three dismounted to let their horses blow.

Johnny said, "Which way now, Rebecca?"

Fanning her perspiring face with her bonnet, she pointed northwest, the direction the mountain trended.

Johnny McVay turned slowly to gaze in that direction, but instantly he became alert.

A little farther along the mountain top, a familiar but sickening movement had caught his eye. He reached for his bridle reins.

"Virgil," he said, "you and Rebecca stay here till I find out what they're feeding on."

Rebecca stopped fanning and pushed a lock of damp, curly hair away from her forehead. "Go with him, Pa."

"Leave the pack horse, then, Virgil."

Johnny's big gray kept a couple of lengths ahead as the two men rode on among the trees. All at once they both reined in, staring transfixed.

Not far ahead the branches of a huge old oak were bent under the weight of buzzards whose long, bare necks writhed from side to side, like snakes. A second later the tree shivered as though struck by a windstorm. With a mighty flapping and threshing and croaking, the buzzards took to the sky.

The ground beneath the oak had been black with them, too. Hopping and flapping, some of the critters had to disgorge the contents of their stomachs before getting aloft. They circled noisily barely above the treetops, and got higher and higher into the hot blue sky.

Touching his gray with a rowel, Johnny went closer. He stared horror-struck at the beak- and fang-mangled remains of Deputy Wade Smollet.

He looked around at Casper and said, "Wait till Uncle Oscar hears about this."

The sound of Rebecca's approaching mare reached them.

"Go back and wait for us," Johnny called.

"No, come on, daughter," Casper said. He lowered his tone. "Let her see this, so she'll get that murdering young devil out of her mind."

Rebecca drew rein.

"We've found what's left of Deputy Smollet," Johnny called. "Hadn't you better go stay with the pack horse?"

Rebecca glanced up through the branches at the circling buzzards. She said then, "I can stand anything you can, Johnny."

He motioned her on.

Wolves had gotten here before the buzzards, shredding Smollet's clothing and scattering it wide. The deputy's boots and spurs were missing and so were his guns.

Casper said, "I believe that scutter would have swapped clothes, if Smollet's had fit."

Stiff-lipped and pale as she sat her saddle, Rebecca said, "Johnny, it'll kill that poor woman if you pack these bones back to her."

Johnny walked over beside Rebecca, looking up at her. "You heard a shot. You came back and found Sammy Lee here with the gun, and Wade Smollet was dead?"

Rebecca shook her head. "Mr. Smollet was still alive. Sammy Lee shot him again. See that hole in the skull yonder? That's where."

Suddenly Rebecca slapped a hand to her mouth and bent sidewise in her saddle away from Johnny, eyes wide. The noxious stench from the gnawed bones and hide of the deputy's horse had caused her nausea.

"Get gone," Johnny said.

The girl meekly obeyed.

Looking at Casper, Johnny said, "She's right about it. Be worse to take Wade's bones to town than to leave them here. Let's get them together and bury them under a pile of rocks."

When the job was done, Johnny took a daybook and stub pencil from the upper right pocket of his vest. He wrote hurriedly, explaining the contents of the cairn. He then put the message under the heavy rock that topped the pile.

Afterward he inspected the deputy's riding gear.

Casper said, "Wolves and coyotes have ruined everything, Johnny. Ain't worth packing in."

"Well," Johnny said, "you and I have done all we can do. Let's go."

It was up to the professional manhunters now.

Johnny had found a finger ring and the deputy's watch, and this was all that Lucy would see. Of course, if Sammy Lee was caught and brought to trial, Bedford Polk would be interested in this cairn. Likely he would want Wade's bullet-riddled skull for evidence.

Joining Casper's daughter, they descended to the spring, quenched their thirst and rested.

"I'm in a hurry to get back to Grief Hill," Johnny said then. "The quickest way will be to follow the mountain to the bend of Goose Creek and cut across to the Fiddleback road. But maybe I'd better go back with you folks."

"We can make it alone. Rebecca did."

"Well, take my carbine. This six-shooter is all I need."

Rebecca said, "Pa, let's divide up the bread and meat with him."

"I'll take some bread and grease and salt."

"You'll take some coffee, too, and a cup and the blanket."

While he tied the blanket and contents behind his saddle cantle, Rebecca came over to him and looked up at his chin. She started to speak.

"Forget it," Johnny said.

Casper scratched his neck. "No need of telling you to be careful, is there, Johnny?"

Johnny gave him a straight look. "I'm going to town, Virgil."

"Thought maybe you'd changed your mind about Sammy Lee."

Johnny shook his head. He said then, "Don't you and Rebecca get sociable with anyone. If somebody tries to get close, wave him around. If he won't wave, take a shot at him. Savvy?"

Casper cut a quick glance at his daughter and nodded.

Later, from a bluff several miles to the south,

Johnny caught a glimpse of the girl and her father far out on the prairie. He rolled a smoke and watched them until a ridge blocked sight of them, and he still wasn't satisfied. He could have been wrong in his snap judgment of Rebecca. She might make a cowhand the best wife imaginable.

Riding on, Johnny turned his thoughts to the dead deputy, and of all that had happened during his sojourn in this valley, he considered the bushwhacking of Smollet the worst. Barlow Clesson's murder or even Johnny's shooting of Joe Hooker was nothing compared with that.

At sundown, near the headwaters of Big Goose Creek, Johnny McVay stopped to unsaddle the gray and stake him out. He built a fire and made some thick black coffee. He broiled bacon on a stick, ate the Caspers' biscuits, then relaxed on the blanket and waited for his horse to graze.

At dusk he saddled up, following the creek down to the prairie. When the stream bent away from the mountain, Johnny knew he was near the Hooker place. It was a couple of hours after sunrise when he crossed to the southside.

Emerging from the bottoms, he put the gray up a long slant. When he reached the crest of the divide, he was three miles east of the wooded bluff that overlooked Hooker's ranch buildings. He rode straight ahead, dropping down into the brushy draw.

Climbing onto rolling rangeland, he rode southeast, to strike the Fiddleback-Grief Hill road. He had ridden less than a mile when his roving gaze settled on a band of mounted men who sat their saddles on the brow of a hill. Continuing, Johnny saw the riders string out down the hillside as if to intercept him. Another elevation hid them for a time. When Johnny saw them again, they were close, bearing down upon him.

Chris Hogarth jerked his horse onto its haunches, stopping quite a way back.

The other five men fanned out to confront Johnny McVay in a semicircle. All wore bullhide chaps. All were clean-shaven and bleak of visage. McVickers was scowling. Clete Maisie's light gray eyes were motionless. Marked by a narrow black mustache, Hogarth's high-cheekboned countenance was a mask of fury.

He said, "Connie warned you not to move onto this ranch!"

"I'm not moving onto it. I'm just in a hurry to reach Grief Hill. The sheriff sent me to track down Wade Smollet. I found him bushwhacked."

Maisie said, "Don't let him weasel out of it, Chris."

Hogarth drew his six-shooter. Walking his horse closer, he eared back the hammer.

Maisie said, "When you throw talk around, you're expected to make good on it. The boys will lose confidence. Shoot him and be done with it, Chris."

"Wait, Hogarth! Maisie is hoping I'll draw and maybe get you. He doesn't care about me. He wants you. I'm not touching my gun."

Maisie lifted his reins. "Let's go, boys. Chris is just loud-mouthed."

Johnny McVay said, "Hogarth, you—" and in this instant Chris Hogarth's gun exploded. Johnny McVay didn't hear it. He didn't see the flame and smoke. He didn't feel the slug in his chest. He toppled from the saddle, jerking the gray's mouth painfully; then the reins slipped from his fingers and he himself seemed to rocket down a long black tunnel. . . .

CHAPTER X

When Johnny McVay came to, he heard himself gagging and coughing, and each time he coughed, a wiry-edged pain gouged through his upper body. He heard Tom Saxon say, "That's enough, Cade. Be a shame to drown him with liquor after he survived the bullet."

Cade Brewster said, "He'll start swallowing in a minute."

Johnny McVay did start swallowing, all the whisky Brewster would let him have.

He opened his eyes and moved his gaze from side to side. Bare to the waist and bandaged below the ribs, he was on a bed, propped up by folded soogans and blankets. The heavy brass bedstead, that had been rolled into the center of the room, seemed familiar. The tawny-haired Saxon was standing at the foot of it. Burly Cade Brewster, holding the whisky bottle, was leaning forward in a chair on Johnny's right. Vern Masefield stood a little farther back. Pete Creighton's swarthy face was visible behind the lantern he held on Johnny's left.

"Hooker ranch?"

Thumbs hooked in his kipskin vest, Saxon nodded. "Who plugged you? We heard the shot but didn't get there quick enough."

"Hogarth."

"Well, you'll put one in him before it's over. And hurry up and get out of that bed. I need you."

"You bought this place?"

"I'm going to run it for Treva."

"I wouldn't ride for you, Saxon."

"Well, then, you be *segundo*, and I'll ride for you —just so Treva gets a toehold here and keeps it."

"She didn't think much of that idea when I mentioned it to her."

"She didn't know how I felt about it."

Johnny closed his eyes. He opened them again when he heard the tawny-haired man move.

Saxon said, "Where were you going?"

Johnny explained about the Caspers and Sammy Lee Dilts and Wade Smollet.

"Oscar ought to know that," Saxon said then. "I'll light a shuck for town and tell him."

"Tell him I stopped a bullet, but that you didn't see it happen. He doesn't have to know all of my business."

"Whatever you say, Johnny." Saxon tugged at the brim of his snake-banded hat. He turned to Brewster. "Take care of things."

"Then you tell them fellers in the bunkhouse I'm in full charge, just the same as if I was foreman."

"You are in full charge. When the wagons get

here, put those fellows to work. Won't hurt them to bend their backs a little."

The tawny-haired man turned out of the bedroom then, his ivory-handled six-shooter bobbing at his hip. And Johnny McVay went back to sleep.

Daylight was outside the windows when he awakened. A warm breeze wafted in on him, bringing sounds of men and horses, familiar routine ranch sounds which heralded a bright new day. Cade Brewster was still in the chair at the bedside.

"Am I shot in the stomach?"

Brewster uncrossed his heavy legs, spurs tinkling, and moved the chair closer. "You'd of knowed it if you was gutshot. We're just hoping it didn't touch your liver or lights."

"I don't feel anything wrong when I breathe."

"Well, kid, that's all there is to it—breathing. Keep at it and you'll live long. Want something? Water, maybe?"

"Water, yes," Johnny said. He was sleeping again soon.

Sometime later he heard the crack of whips and the shouting of teamsters, but he didn't fully arouse. When he did awaken to rational thoughts, Cade Brewster was spooning broth into his mouth.

Brewster said, "I figured this would bring you around."

"I heard the supply wagons."

"That was yesterday. Tom brought this broth from town. Treva fixed it for you. She stayed in town, but aims for you to get well fast, just like Tom does. Are you aiming to keep awake now?"

"I'll try to."

Turning his head, Brewster called through the inner doorway, "Pete!"

Bootsteps sounded. An unlighted cigar jutting from his swarthy face, Creighton entered the bedroom.

Brewster said, "Where did Tom and the sheriff get off to?"

"Tom went to see if the cookshack's ready for the new *cocinero*. Rodin went with him, I reckon."

"Go and tell them the kid's awake now, and his fever's gone down."

Creighton went toward the rear of the house and didn't return, but Saxon and Rodin appeared, and Pablo Cardoza came as far as the bedroom door.

Brewster got to his feet and motioned for the sheriff to take the bedside chair.

Saxon stopped at the foot of the bed. A bright law badge had been pinned to his vest. The pocket above the badge held a row of cigars which the tawny-haired man had been passing out.

Sheriff Rodin had one. He leaned forward to peer at his nephew's features. "Uh-huh, you got shot right where you drilled Joe Hooker, didn't you?"

"Almost. But not for the same reason."

Saxon said, "Johnny'll be able to sit up by tomorrow, Oscar, long enough to get him to town."

"Be reasonable," Johnny said. "I couldn't ride that far."

Sheriff Rodin said, "You don't know what you can do till you have to. Pablo brought Tyndale's buggy. If we don't get you to where the doctor can tend to you, you might not pull through, though it looks like these fellers are pretty good sawbones, theirselves."

"Johnny was in good shape," Saxon said.

"Uh-huh. Johnny, I moved you out of the hotel. Leastwise I rented you a room from Lucy. You was on an errand for the county, and she'll get paid for taking care of you."

"Bet you hated to tell her about Wade."

"Well, I took Brother Phillips and Doc Mueller and Tom, here, with me. Lucy took it right hard, but she'll have to go on and make the best of it, just like all of us. I recollect when them cussed Comanches . . ." The sheriff looked out the window, voice trailing off.

Johnny said, "Saxon bought Brewster's broncs and aims to run cattle."

"Uh-huh. You ain't jealous of Tom's badge, are you? You couldn't hold down Wade's job, and

Steve couldn't even maintain order and law in Grief Hill, let alone the county. Tom's all I had to turn to. I ast him, and he said he would move back to town."

"What about this place?"

Saxon said, "We intend for you to take over here. You will, because Treva plans to make it worth your while."

Johnny didn't comment. He only closed his eyes.

Sheriff Rodin said, "Here now, Johnny, wake up. I have to know where you was when Sammy Lee plugged you, so's I can pick up his trail."

Johnny looked at Saxon accusingly.

Saxon shrugged. "What did you expect him to think?"

Sheriff Rodin's eyes sharpened. "How's that, boys? It wasn't something betwixt you fellers, was it?"

Saxon shook his head.

Rodin said, "Well, I don't calculate on being gone long. I've done wired everybody I could think of. You'll probably get answers, and you just relay them on to me when you hear from me. Dilts ain't had much owlhoot practice, so he shouldn't be hard to catch."

Saxon put a cigar into his mouth and rolled it from side to side. "Even if you're gone a year, Oscar, your office will be taken care of. And I'll be on the job."

"Or dead," Johnny McVay pointed out.

Tom Saxon chuckled. He said to the others, "That bullet gave Johnny a serious turn of mind, didn't it?"

It was another twenty-four hours before Cade Brewster, who'd had wartime experience with gunshot wounds, would permit Johnny McVay to leave the bed. Putting Johnny in a chair, he brought water and shaving tools and scraped his face, and helped him into his clothes and boots. Masefield had washed and darned the shirt and vest. Saxon and Brewster helped him out to the buggy, which contained his saddle and other gear. The gray was tied behind. Masefield accompanied Saxon as outrider, and Pablo Cardoza tooled the dappled team.

He followed the trail along the base of the barranca to the edge of the Hooker land. Running east was an old road that Saxon's wagons had rutted recently. When it reached the open range, it merged with the trail from the Fiddleback.

Johnny McVay squinted into the sunshine as they rolled east, and he found it painfully bright.

Later in the day he imagined himself back in Wyoming, and someone was accusing him of being delirious. He knew when they stopped under the lone tree near the Grief Hill bridge. Although weak and feverish, he was aware of reaching Lucy Smollet's house—the only one with morning-glory vines. He heard himself talking with Lucy, and it made him downright happy when they got him into a bedroom and pulled his boots off.

Lucy was alone in the room when he asked, "Where's my gun?"

She took his hand and placed it on the familiar butt of the Remington. She said then, "I'll hang it on the bedpost, Johnny. Here at the foot."

"I can't reach."

"I'll hand it to you."

Later Tom Saxon's voice said, "If you need anything, Lucy, send for it and charge it to me or Johnny. Need money, write a check. It'll be covered."

"You're a good man, Tom."

After a silence, Tom Saxon said heavily, "I can't always make Treva believe that, Lucy."

"Well, you will. Just keep trying."

They left the room together.

Sometime after that, feeling Lucy adjusting the pillow, Johnny asked, "How's Mike?"

"Sassy as ever. He's in yonder on a pallet, Johnny. Don't you hear him pounding that bottle on the floor?"

Doctor Mueller arrived, talking with Lucy in broken English and leaving a medicinal smell in the room, along with a bottle of bitter-tasting stuff for Johnny to screw up his face over.

During the days following, Steve Fenwick

came, wearing a new Stetson he'd bought with some of the Minch reward money, and he kept it on in the house.

Bedford Polk was with Tom Saxon when he drew a chair up beside the bed and asked, "Who shot you, Johnny?"

"Hogarth."

"A fair shake?"

"I couldn't even beg him not to."

Polk's crowfooted eyes were serious, his tone placating. "I'll get out a warrant for assault and have Tom bring him to town. See what the court can do to him. If I do that, you won't go gunning for him, will you?"

"I don't know. It was a pretty rotten deal."

Polk studied him a moment and then asked for details concerning the bushwhacking of Smollet, stopping Johnny once before Lucy appeared. The attorney and the deputy left together, talking about a posse. Johnny didn't feel like thinking about it now.

In the cool of the evening he went out to a rocker on Lucy's front porch, sitting there behind the vines and listening to the noises of the town. Near sundown he heard someone at the gate and started to rise to see past the morning-glory vines. But Lucy's moccasins scuffed from the living room.

She said, "Come in, Brother Phillips."

The black-clad young minister reached the

steps, asking, "How's your patient, Mrs. Smollet?"

"Why, he's doing right well, Billy. He's sitting up." Lucy gestured.

Johnny said, "How are you, Reverend?"

"Oh, same as usual, Johnny." The preacher took a nearby chair. "I believe you've lost a little weight. Look kind of peaked."

"I could stand to lose some."

Lucy said, "Billy, you made a trip down Goose Creek, didn't you?"

"Yes, ma'am. I just got back."

"Are you holding a revival meeting down there?"

"I'm going to. If we can get an arbor built, I plan to open one next Monday." The minister turned again to Johnny McVay. "The Casper family asked about you. They said if your condition was critical, they'd get someone to look after their livestock, and come to town. I told them that Dr. Mueller said you were in no danger."

"Did Rebecca send any word to me?"

The young minister smiled. "She said for you to watch the coffeepots."

"I guess folks tell preachers everything."

"Some of them do. Virgil sent your horse and saddle. I gave Pablo your rifle."

"I'm obliged to you."

Still smiling, the preacher said, "That isn't enough. I'll expect you to be in my congregation when you're able to attend."

"Stuck off on a ranch, a man hasn't got much time for church."

"All the more reason to attend now. It's best to keep the Lord on your side, Johnny. Isn't that right, Mrs. Smollet?"

Arms folded, Lucy was between their chairs, leaning against the wall. Expression guarded, she said, "Well, Wade and I had been pretty steady churchgoers. But it's hard to understand sometimes, Billy."

The preacher nodded. "It could be that Wade's lost years will be accorded to Mike, Mrs. Smollet, the remainder of his three score and ten."

"I sure hope so," Lucy said fervently, and then she added, "Billy, you reminded me of something. I've got some didies to wash. You boys make yourselves at home."

"Lucy," Johnny said, "I'm thinking of taking a walk down to the plaza."

"You ain't going to do no such a thing. Don't you step foot outside that gate. You're not as strong as you think you are."

"When can I go?"

"Tomorrow, maybe. We'll wait and see." Lucy went into the living room.

Johnny McVay told the Reverend Phillips then, "It's been years since I've heard a good sermon, and that might be just what I need."

CHAPTER XI

No one in Grief Hill could sleep with the windows down and the doors shut, trapping inside the house the sultry summer heat. Lucy Smollet's house was wide open. No low-turned lamp was burning. Johnny McVay no longer needed attention during the night. The bedroom was in darkness, therefore, when Johnny suddenly awakened. Only a sound could have aroused him. At this moment all he heard were two broncs at the nearby public livery stable. The noise they made indicated something Johnny had witnessed many a time: two mustangs had swung their hindquarters toward each other and were pitching and kicking and squealing.

"Mrs. Smollet?" The voice was that of a man apparently hailing Lucy from the front gate.

In the dark Lucy emerged from her bedroom, softly pulling the door to, and crossed the living room. She then spoke in a low tone so as not to arouse her sleeping child.

"Who are you and what do you want?"

A familiar girl's voice answered. "It's Connie Clesson. I was told Johnny McVay lives here."

"Yes, he does. And if you Fiddlebackers are looking for more trouble, you'll sure get it. Wade made me one of the best shots in this town."

"It's just Vic McVickers and I," Connie pleaded. "May I come in?"

"Well, I guess so, if you won't wake up my baby."

Johnny McVay had gotten out of bed and by the time Lucy had lit the lamps and approached his room, he was dressed.

He said, "I heard her, Lucy. I'll be right there."

Pausing only to grab the brush off the dresser and take a few swipes at his hair, he followed Lucy's footsteps. The redheaded widow had pulled a robe on over her nightgown and had seated Connie on the couch. Connie's shingled, blond head was bare. Her trim figure was encased in a becoming street dress, but her cheeks were flushed and her eyes smoldered with antagonism.

Looking from one to the other, Lucy said, "I'll let you two talk."

"Don't go, unless your baby needs you. I never did tell you how much I appreciate Mr. Smollet's making the long ride the night my father was killed."

"He was a good man," Lucy murmured.

Johnny had taken a chair near the couch. Succeeding in keeping her emotions under control, Connie said to him, "You think you're going to shove me back and take what you want, but you're not."

"You Fiddlebackers think you're going to get rid of me, too, but you're not."

"Connie," Lucy said wearily, "if you woke us up just to quarrel, you've sure got your gall."

Connie gestured with both hands. "This man here, this nephew of the county sheriff, has thrown in with Tom Saxon and Eric Veblen and goodness knows who else to fight the Fiddleback."

"Well, Connie, I always said the day would come when folks would stop saying their prayers to you people."

Connie involuntarily sat erect, gaze darting about as though she were cornered. Sinking back onto the couch, she said to Johnny, "Wish I had known what sort of man you were."

"I'm not one who'll pull out just because he's told to. Pass that on to your foreman, will you? Tell Hogarth I've got a crow to pick with him, and he'd better be ready."

Connie watched him tensely for a moment, pulse throbbing at her throat. Leaning back against the couch, she placed a hand to her heart.

Alarmed, Lucy said, "Girl, what's got you so excited?"

"Chris Hogarth is dead, Mrs. Smollet. Tom Saxon killed him. But I can see now that Johnny wasn't in on it. He didn't even know it."

Lucy said, "You loved Chris."

"Yes. Yes, I did."

Tom Saxon, the girl explained, had ridden up to the Fiddleback headquarters with six men he claimed were posse members. He showed a deputy sheriff's badge and said that Oscar Rodin had left him in full charge. He had a warrant for Chris, because of Johnny.

"I told Chris we had more money than blood, and he agreed not to fight but to submit to arrest. I started to send some men back with the posse, but Saxon wouldn't permit it. Said he didn't trust us. He promised to bring a letter to Owen Tyndale, though, and we let him have Chris. About an hour later, they brought Chris back, dead. *Ley de fuga*, Saxon said."

"Law of escape," Lucy murmured.

Johnny said, "I'll bet Clete Maisie was pleased."

"What?"

"I don't think Clete Maisie liked your foreman."

"Clete doesn't like anyone much. But he's loyal to the brand. Barlow said he was the most loyal man in our *corrida*."

After a moment, Johnny said, "Well, I wish I could sympathize with you, but Hogarth shot me like a sitting duck. He got his needings."

Connie lowered her gaze, lacing fingers in her lap, the lighted flower-painted globe of the table lamp gleaming on the cut-shell buttons of her dress.

Lucy said, "What do you expect Johnny to do?"

"Nothing. I wouldn't have come here if I had known he had actually nothing to do with

Hogarth's death." Her mouth twisted. "When Tom Saxon takes that badge off, he'll wish he hadn't killed Chris—if he has time to wish anything."

"Did Maisie say he would get him?" Johnny asked.

"Clete didn't, but the rest of them did. Tom Saxon is a marked man." Frowning and silent, Connie then said, "I talked with Treva. She blubbered about it. Said Tom shouldn't have done it. I tried to make a deal with her again, but she said it was too late."

"How big is your Fiddleback crew?" Johnny asked.

"Oh, I don't know how many we have right now. They come and go. Barlow always kept twelve in the bunkhouse through the winter and I'll do the same."

Lucy said, "Is Treva going to marry Tom?"

"I didn't ask her."

"Well, she would have to go a long way to find a better man than Tom Saxon."

"That's where you and I disagree, Mrs. Smollet. And he won't make a very good bridegroom when he comes out from behind that tin badge."

Johnny said, "I don't see why you keep fighting for something that isn't really yours. Your claim to the Hooker place wouldn't stand up in court."

"My father bought it and paid for it."

"You keep saying that, Connie, but I can't

uncover any records at the courthouse to back you up. Barlow was never slipshod in any other deals."

"Well, he was like a lot of other people. Sorry for Joe on account of Treva's mother leaving him for Eric Veblen." Connie got to her feet again. "When I came here, I thought Johnny was helping Tom Saxon use the sheriff's office against me. I'll let you go back to bed now."

Lucy told her good night and followed her to the steps, waiting until McVickers had driven her away.

Johnny McVay couldn't go back to sleep immediately. He mulled over the care he had received at the Hooker ranch house. Cade Brewster had seemed genuinely concerned about Johnny's wound, yet maybe it was because the Fiddleback had inflicted it. Masefield and Creighton's solicitude had been genuine, though. Finally, Johnny drifted off into a troubled sleep. . . .

The sun had risen, and the blacksmith was already at work in his nearby shop when Johnny went into the kitchen to build a fire. He had coffee ready when Lucy appeared, red hair tousled, sleep still in her eyes.

She said, "I could have done without that visit from Connie last night," and continued on to the back porch.

"Did Mike keep you awake?" Johnny asked when she returned.

"No, it wasn't Mike. I was just thinking. About Wade and Oscar and Sammy Lee Dilts. He might bushwhack Oscar, too."

Johnny was pouring two cups of coffee. "Don't worry about that. Nothing would please Uncle Oscar better than having Sammy Lee try it. What I'm afraid of is that Uncle Oscar will collar Sammy Lee somewhere when they're all alone. The best Sammy Lee could hope for then would be a bullet. Uncle Oscar might hang him right then and there."

"Oscar's a fool about Mike," Lucy said, and after a moment added moodily, "Sometime when Mike gets bigger, I want to visit that cairn on the mountain."

They finished their second cups of coffee, and Lucy pushed back her chair. "I'd better get some breakfast started."

"And I'll chop some wood and draw some water if you're going to wash today."

Lucy stood on the porch and watched Johnny's face as he drew the first bucket, making sure he hadn't overestimated his strength. Presently she called to him, "I'm taking down your yellow flag. You're not quarantined anymore. You can do as you please."

"About time."

An hour later Johnny strapped on his gunbelt and left the house. His first stop was the barbershop for a shave and haircut, then he hunted up

Pablo Cardoza, sending him to get the made-to-order saddle. Men stopped Johnny here and there, wanting a first-hand account of the search for Deputy Smollet, of Johnny's own slug through the brisket, and of Connie Clesson's reaction to the death of her foreman.

Johnny was on the plaza, among the onlookers at the horseshoe game, when Owen Tyndale walked up beside him.

"Busy, Johnny?"

Johnny said, "No," and followed the attorney away from the crowd. After they had walked beyond earshot, Tyndale waited for Johnny to catch up.

"Are you going to stay here, or are you going back to Wyoming?"

"Far as I know now, I'm staying here."

"Good. In about an hour you come up to Eric Veblen's office."

"Mind telling me what for?"

"He'll tell you," Tyndale said, and after studying Johnny McVay's blond features narrowly, he walked off under the trees, apparently headed for the courthouse.

Marshal Fenwick walked up, his florid face wreathed with a grin. "What's that shyster up to?"

"Sucking me into something I won't like, I expect."

"Better watch him." Marshal Fenwick lifted

and reset his new Stetson. "You didn't quite get gutshot out there on the Hooker place, and he ain't satisfied."

"Tyndale isn't my enemy."

Marshal Fenwick sobered. "No, I don't reckon." His features became worried. "But I'll tell you who is, Johnny—Tom Saxon. With that deputy badge pinned to his chest, he's swelling up bigger and bigger. It's over two years till election. Now, if Oscar don't make it back, chances are Tom will stay right where he is, holding down Oscar's swivel chair. Then he'll run for sheriff next time."

Johnny stared at him, for some reason becoming angry.

"If Tom sent somebody to dry-gulch Oscar," Fenwick said, "Sammy Lee Dilts would get credit for it, wouldn't he?"

Johnny McVay's brows knitted. "You think Tom Saxon might really do something like that?"

"He likes to wear a badge better'n any man I ever seen."

Still frowning, Johnny said, "Guess I was too close to it to figure it out. What had we better do?"

"Warn Oscar. Send telegrams and write letters to everywhere we can think of. Because if Oscar does keep in touch with Tom, me and you won't know about it. He's holding high cards here now, Tom is."

Johnny said tautly, "We'd better do as you say, this afternoon sometime."

At mid-morning the wagons and teams along the dusty streets, the hipshot horses drowsing in the sunshine in front of the business establishments, and the occasional strings of pack mules winding down out of the hills to the east, marked Grief Hill for what it was—the supply center for the valley and a wide area beyond.

Johnny McVay found the Silver Saddle Saloon thronged. The perfessor was pounding the ivories, sharp-eyed hopefuls were wooing Lady Luck at the gambling layouts and two bartenders were hustling to serve the men bellied up at the mahogany.

Johnny dragged his spurs through the sawdust to the stairway. He laid a hand on a polished newelpost and glanced up at the mezzanine, observing as he climbed that the saloonkeeper's office door was open.

Veblen was seated in the high-backed padded chair behind the flat-topped desk. Crossing the few feet of balcony, Johnny stepped through the doorway onto the rug, and the fat saloonkeeper pushed back his chair and got up. He came from behind the desk.

"Hogarth almost got you, didn't he?"

"Yeah, but it cost him his life."

Veblen said, almost accusingly, "You tried to talk your way out of it."

"I won't make that mistake again," Johnny said. He moved around to the chair which Veblen always kept near his own.

"Facing that man," Veblen said, "I would probably have turned tail and run."

"And got it in the back."

Veblen nodded. "Likely." He put his hands in his pockets. "Hogarth's slug was really meant for Tom. He thought you had moved onto the Hooker place."

"Well, Tom made sure he didn't get a chance to correct it."

Veblen moved his expensively clad bulk around the office. He came back and sat down, turning his chair to face Johnny.

"You've got Tom figured wrong," he said, and appeared hesitant, as though he wanted to speak further but doubted the wisdom of it.

"How's that?"

Veblen said, "Tom likes you, Johnny."

"Maybe that's because I'm Oscar Rodin's nephew. Tom likes that badge he's wearing."

"You pistol-whipped him, and that's hard for any man to overlook, especially when his friends saw it. But he's not holding any grudge. I'll bet my bottom dollar on it."

"He shouldn't. He asked for it. And that reminds me, you tried to throw him downstairs. Is he nursing a grudge over that?"

Veblen grunted. After a moment, he said, "Tom

could have shot me if he'd wanted to. I had a gun on. He knew it."

"It looked as though he got out of it the only way he could. Disarmed himself. Backed water."

Veblen shook his head. "You don't quite understand."

"What are you leading up to, Eric?"

"Treva." The saloonkeeper turned to the desk and pulled out a drawer. He took some papers from it. "I had Owen make these out. They're partnership papers. These will give you a half-interest in the Hooker ranch."

"Think I can make it worth something?"

"If you can't, I don't know who could."

Johnny made an impatient gesture. "It's not worth a dang, Eric. A man would have to cut that Fiddleback crew for gunfighters before throwing cattle onto that range. Putting cattle on that grass will be a lot harder than moving in a few sticks of furniture."

"You'd be afraid to try?"

"Tom Saxon's aiming to try, isn't he? If Treva figures he isn't big enough, let her take the preacher in as partner."

Veblen smiled. "Billy was my idea, not hers. They're all through now."

"Is she through with Tom?"

"No, but he won't cause you any trouble."

Veblen extended a box of choice Havanas. They both took one and lit up. With fragrant smoke curling before him, Johnny said, "Connie Clesson told me that Treva blubbered about Hogarth."

"It scared her. She knows Fiddleback will try to get revenge on Tom, sooner or later. She thinks you might keep them from it. That's why she wanted this partnership deal." Veblen paused. "It'll have to be strictly business, though."

Johnny McVay flushed. "Sounds like I've been pushing myself on her."

The jowled saloonkeeper watched him intently.

Johnny said, "If I did take a partnership in that place, I wouldn't want to be bothered by Tom Saxon. Wouldn't even want him around."

"Anything you say. But he's already got you bested with Treva."

"I'll take my chances. How does the deal go?"

Veblen looked worried, but he passed Johnny the documents. "Your cow savvy against her ironclad title. You match her dollar for dollar in stocking the range." He leaned back in the chair. "When you said you could borrow money, you put it mildly. I had you looked up. That Scotsman your mother married has a potful."

"He made it in the cattle business. What else showed up about me?"

"You got thimblerigged out of seventeen thousand dollars, and your stepfather had to make it good."

Johnny's chin came up, teeth set in the cigar. "Wait a minute, now. I sold off a herd of my own to pay him back. That's why I was free to come down here."

"You don't gamble now."

Johnny shook his head. "Not on the other fellow's game." He gestured with the documents. "Like this, for instance."

Veblen thumbed his chin. "But this is your game, isn't it? You told Joe Hooker you'd do it, when Joe was dying. Tom's moved in supplies and bought a remuda, but there's nothing out there you won't need. We can work it all out."

"Give Tom his money back?"

"Let's let it ride for a while till we see how you and Tom hit it off."

Johnny said, "Treva does just about what you tell her to, doesn't she?"

Vablen shifted his huge body and straightened his legs. "She does now, but she didn't used to. I didn't know how to manage her. Our housekeeper changed that. She told me, 'Eric, when you know you're right, make that girl toe the line. Don't you want her to respect you?'" Veblen sat with his chin down, lost in reflection. Presently he said, "I laid awake many a night after Treva's mother died, worrying about a saloonkeeper raising someone else's little daughter."

"You don't have to pretend with me, Eric.

Nothing wrong with you as a father, except maybe not enough exercise."

"And too big an appetite. And being short on brains. I'll tell you something, Johnny, but you don't have to believe it. Jay Minch showed me a derringer in a sleeve clip one day. When I had my quarrel with him over Barlow Clesson, I thought he was carrying that hideout gun. The look in Jay's eyes—*he* thought he was carrying it."

Johnny nodded. "Minch disremembered leaving it in his room and made a move for it. I see what you mean, Eric. I always decide by a man's eyes whether to shoot him. It's the only way you can tell when you mess with the top-notchers."

Stabbing a finger at the papers, Veblen said, "Treva's already signed them. Let's go downstairs and get a couple of witnesses, and you sign them. And have a drink on it."

Eyes squinted, teeth clamped on the cigar, Johnny considered it. He said, "Guess you'll always be handy when I need advice."

"It depends on how well you get along with Tom and Treva. Did you know Tom has a new team and buggy?"

Johnny shook his head.

"Yeah. A team of sorrels that cost him seven-fifty. He and Treva are off somewhere right now." Veblen was eyeing Johnny closely.

"Well," Johnny said, "he's good company,

I reckon. Good-looking and easygoing, when he wants to be. Born with a silver spoon in his mouth. Probably pretty hard to say no to him."

Treva and Tom were still on Johnny McVay's mind when he left the saloon. He crossed to the well and got a drink and wet his face. Continuing on to the bank corner, he stood there, and finally he espied Saxon's new buggy approaching from the south. The tawny-haired man was holding the sorrels to an amble.

Estimating the distance, Johnny angled toward the Emporium and reached the middle of the street in time to step in front of the team.

Saxon stopped the sorrels and gave Johnny a bright, speculative look. He was bareheaded. Doffing his Stetson, Johnny went around to Treva's side of the buggy.

He said, "Tom's a deputy sheriff now, and ought to be attending to that business. You and I have a ranch to talk about."

He held out his hand.

Treva didn't take it to alight from the buggy. Framed by a bonnet and hair of blackest black, her pretty features were serene. She scooted closer to Saxon and held her skirt.

"Get in, Johnny. We'll go up home. Ross can bring you back to town."

Johnny looked at Saxon. "Are you going to visit a while?"

Saxon smiled. "I can't. I left Steve Fenwick in the office, and he needs sleep."

"Well, I guess I can go," Johnny said, and got into the rig, again inhaling a whiff of Treva's sachet and once more wondering if Connie Clesson, up close, had such a citified stink.

CHAPTER XII

Seeming to cleave the summit of the mountain, a spiral of lightning hurtled from the zenith, while smaller spirals shot out on either side; the illusion was that of a jagged lightning trunk with flat and jagged branches. The heavens were black afterward.

Forking his gelding and the saddle he had ridden into this valley, Johnny McVay opened his jaws to revive his hearing after the terrific thunderclap had slammed away from the mountain, and as thunder growled and rumbled in the distance, he watched a tall tree up there become a flaming torch.

The rain would be a gully-washer when it came.

A while back Johnny had stopped to empty his pockets of everything he wanted to keep dry, and had rolled the stuff in his slicker, tying it behind the cantle. As for himself, he hoped to get wet. Nothing would be more pleasant than getting soaked in a downpour. Expecting to own half the cattle that would fatten on grass hereabouts, what man could cuss a rainstorm?

The tree on the mountain kept burning.

Johnny had discussed everything he could think of with Treva, there in the Veblen parlor, and her reply had been, "Whatever you say, Johnny. I don't know anything about ranching," and he had told her, "But I want to please you," then she'd said, "I'm not hard to please."

The fact was, however, Johnny couldn't savvy the girl. It was a vague something he couldn't quite corner in his mind, but it was there, and because he couldn't pin it down, it started eating into him. Maybe, as time passed, he would begin to understand her. Actually, though, to be honest with himself, his heart wasn't in it. Perhaps it was because, deep down inside, he felt that Connie Clesson was in the right, not Treva.

Ascending the brushy draw, Johnny put the gelding through the motte of trees skirting the willows of the marshy water hole and riding on toward the corner of the bluff. Not a drop of rain had fallen yet, but Johnny could smell it. The next big streak of lightning would doubtless bring it sluicing down.

Johnny had asked Treva what brand to register, suggesting a Double T. Her eyes had gleamed momentarily in a way that had puzzled him then, and it puzzled him now. Such a brand would be fine, she'd said.

Johnny's gaze was on the flickering tree-torch up there above the barranca, but in his mind's eye he was viewing the Hooker ranch headquarters as it had looked from the blackjacks yonder, atop the escarpment. He was visualizing the ell-shaped ranch house, the long bunkhouse, the square cookshack, three nice barns and lean-tos, several sheds. He recalled the wide expanse of corrals, the stretch of meadow the Fiddleback had been cutting hay from. The hay meadow and access to Big Goose Creek were really the prizes the Fiddleback would fight for, not the set of buildings.

Johnny rode on past the bluff. When he put the gelding onto the alluvial fan, the ranch house was in darkness, so he angled in front of it and rode toward the lighted windows of the bunkhouse, a hundred yards farther down.

He dismounted at the hitch rack and wrapped a rein around the pole. Shifting his Remington .44 to its accustomed place, he turned to the doorway and stepped into the lamplighted room, pushing back his low-crowned hat.

Two men at the table, bumping heads with a deck of cards, looked at him. One was the swarthy Pete Creighton, who asked, "Did Tom come with you, Johnny?"

"No."

A man lying with his face to the rear wall rolled over on his bunk. He was old Vern Masefield, and got to his feet, fingering his grizzled hair.

"Where's Cade?" Johnny asked.

Vern said, "I don't know, if he ain't down at the cookshack." Gesturing at a rear window, he said, "I was laying here watching a glow on the rim.

169

That big flash of lightning must have set a tree on fire."

A man in the south end of the room said, "I thought it hit this cussed bunkhouse."

"You sure could smell it," another said.

Johnny looked from one man to another, showing due interest, and then said, "Well, I want to see Cade," and went back outside.

Mounting, he rode on the short distance to the lighted cookshack, fat raindrops splashing off his hat, thunder rumbling in the distance. Farther on were the corrals, now filled with horses. Beyond them were the meadow and Big Goose. Johnny ground-tied the gelding, got his slicker, and entered the cookshack to find Cade Brewster and the cook confronting each other over a checkerboard. They were seated on benches at the long dining table, above which glowed hanging lamps. When they looked at the doorway, Johnny stopped and stared.

The *cocinero* was a chunky man with a sparse thatch of light sorrel hair and a steerhorn mustache.

Coming to the bench Cade was on, Johnny put down his slicker. He said, "Shoo-fly, you old saddle bum, what are you doing here?"

Shoo-fly Flynn appeared disgusted. "What does it look like? This isn't Wyoming, and it's not the Crescent-Two. If you monkey around here, I'll lay a cleaver alongside your head."

"How long you been here?"

"I got here the day you left in that Sunday-go-to-meeting rig. I met you, but Tom couldn't make you recognize me. That's what lead-poisoning does to a kid."

"You haven't been trailing me, I reckon. You left home a couple of months before I did."

The burly Cade Brewster was looking from one to the other, grinning.

Johnny said, "I don't know which is the best checker player, but I know who's the best cook. Cade is. That chuck he force-fed me sure brought me around."

"Tom packed that out from town," Brewster said.

Johnny went back into the kitchen part of the room. "How's the chance for chuck right now, Shoo-fly?"

"Help yourself."

Johnny looked at Brewster. "Where'll I put my horse?"

"I'll take him, kid," Brewster said, and got up from the bench.

Johnny said, "Cade, I noticed you're keeping your remuda corraled at night. Figure the Fiddleback might make a raid?"

"They won't as long as Tom's wearing that deputy sheriff badge. No, I just didn't want the men to have to night hawk. Them horses ain't working, no-how."

Brewster leaned over on braced hands to study the checkerboard. Meeting Shoo-fly's gaze, he said, "I remember where they are, and they'd better be there when I get back."

"I wouldn't steal."

Johnny said derisively, "No, Shoo-fly wouldn't steal. Anything that ain't nailed down, that is."

A clap of thunder shook the building as Cade Brewster went out. Johnny got coffee from the three-gallon pot and beans from the kettle. The bread was gone. Carrying his plate and cup and tools to the table, he sat down near the wall.

Without saying anything, Shoo-fly Flynn got up and went into the rear part of the building. He came back with a raw onion, peeled it and put it on Johnny's plate of beans.

"Ruins the taste of good coffee," he grumbled, "but you never could tell the difference."

Mouth full, Johnny cut a glance at him, then asked, "How come you got off down here in Texas?"

Shoo-fly brushed his mustache. "Tom Saxon was in Abilene looking for a trail cook. He intended to buy some remnant brands, and hired me to help him round them up this winter. When I got down here, he'd changed his mind."

"Have you met Ma's brother, Oscar Rodin?"

Shoo-fly shook his head. "Tom said he had taken out after a killer."

"That man killed Oscar's deputy."

Shoo-fly said, "Well, if he's anything like your ma, your Uncle Oscar won't stop till he gets him."

Johnny drank some of the coffee. "That's right. He'd resign from office to track down Wade Smollet's killer. Wade left a widow and a young one. You heard about Uncle Oscar's family, didn't you?"

"The Comanches, yeah."

Rain was pounding on the roof shakes when Cade Brewster returned. He slapped his wet headpiece down on the bench and bent over the checkerboard. Satisfied his men were all there, he stepped over the bench and sat down.

Johnny McVay made another trip to the stove for more coffee and beans.

"Hear that?" the cook asked.

Johnny said, "Sure. Why don't you go out there and stand in it, Shoo-fly? You're still carrying dust from Abilene. Wyoming, too, probably."

"In my ears, maybe," Shoo-fly admitted, and then he asked, "When are you going home, Johnny?"

"Can't say."

Shoo-fly said glumly, "Wish I was there right now."

"Ain't got nothing against Tom, have you?" Brewster asked.

"Not a thing, except he's plumb lost interest

in the cattle business. That law badge, I expect."

"Well," Brewster said, "like I told you fellers, it saves us a lot of worry."

"That might be the reason Tom pinned it on," Shoo-fly said, "but it's not the only reason. He figures he was cut out to be a peace-officer."

Johnny carried his empty plate and cup and iron eating tools back to the dishpan. Not wanting to unroll his slicker, he borrowed a smoke from Flynn, and sat down near him. He watched the *cocinero* make the winning jump.

Disgustedly, Brewster said, "That's enough for me."

"Shoo-fly didn't beat you, Cade. He stole your men."

"I knowed he was doing it, but I couldn't catch him at it. I believe he can steal one while you're looking straight at it." Stepping over the bench, Brewster picked up his hat. "I've got to go up to the house. May start blowing pretty soon, and I ain't sure the windows are all down."

Shoo-fly said, "Coming back?"

"Not tonight."

Johnny said, "I'll go with you, Cade." He stood up and got his slicker.

The burly man eyed him narrowly. "You got a reason for wanting to get wet?"

"A good one."

"Well, come on."

They hit a high lope through the rain. They passed the lamplighted bunkhouse, trotted on and sprang onto the end of the porch which spanned the ell of the darkened ranch house. They slapped rain off their hats.

"We'll go in here," Brewster said. He unlocked a door and swung it open and warm air gushed against their faces. Brewster said, "These windows are down," and entered the room.

Johnny stood there on the porch and listened to the rain on the roof. Finally he said impatiently, "What are you doing, Cade?"

"Hunting something to dry my hands on."

"Use your shirt tail."

Cade growled then, "Ah, here's that cussed wastebasket." A match flared. The burly man touched the flame to the wick of a bracket lamp at one end of a desk, and said, "Come on in, kid." He moved to light the lamp at the other end of the desk. Turning to the north windows, he pulled down the shades. "I'll go see about the other rooms and be right back. Leave this door open, don't you think?"

"We need some air."

Brewster stepped out onto the porch.

The office was small, but big enough. The wastebasket had eluded Cade because it had been pushed into the leghole of the desk. There were two other chairs beside the one at the desk, and Johnny noticed a wall-rack which held a dozen long-range Remington breach-loaders. He saw a wooden cabinet and a zinc-covered chest, and tossed the slicker onto the chest.

He took his sack of makings and the partnership agreement from the slicker.

When Brewster returned and sat down, Johnny handed the papers to him.

"Tom send them?" Brewster asked.

"Read them."

Using his keys on the desk, Brewster rolled the top up and took a pair of steel-rimmed spectacles from a pigeonhole. He chewed his lip as he read.

Handing the papers back, he said, "Well, kid, I quit as of right now. Me and you wouldn't get along at all."

"We might."

"Not me," Cade said, "I'm lighting a shuck."

"Well, that's laying it on the line, Cade."

Brewster watched him steadily. "In a mixed-up deal like this, I wouldn't ever know who's boss. Tom's wife—"

"Tom's *what?*"

"They didn't tell you? Treva Veblen. Her and Tom got hitched."

Johnny McVay's face hardened.

Brewster said, "Was you hoping you'd get her? Too late now. Tom said when he told Eric about it, he thought Eric was going to have a stroke. Said Eric threw him out of the office and tried to kick him downstairs."

Through taut lips, Johnny said, "I'm glad you told me before I got a lot of money tied up here." Johnny thought about it, face flushed. All at once he and Cade burst out laughing.

Brewster said, "Using herself as bait until she got you in too deep to back out."

"Looks that way."

"As far as I know," Brewster said, "you're the fastest gun-slinger that ever hit this valley. She wants you on Tom's side."

Thunder rumbled in the distance. The drumming of the rain increased. Johnny said, "Well, I'm on his side, but I won't be a partner in this ranch. So you sit tight, Cade, right where you are."

"We'll whip the Fiddleback," Brewster said, "one man at a time, if no other way."

Johnny nodded. "If Tom can keep that badge on and get them like he got Hogarth."

Brewster frowned. "Are you criticizing him? Why, Hogarth came within an inch of sending you to Kingdom Come."

"I'd criticize anyone who arrested a man and took him off and killed him."

Brewster tapped his own chest. "I shot Hogarth, myself. He grabbed Tom's gun, and if Tom hadn't dove out of the saddle, he'd of been a goner."

"Armed men all around and Hogarth had that much guts?"

The burly man looked disgusted. "You don't know what you're talking about. We met Clete Maisie. He asked to talk with Hogarth, private. Tom told him to take his six-shooters off. He gave Tom his belt. Him and Hogarth rode out of earshot and powwowed. They came back. Clete was strapping on his guns and we was all watching him. Tom yelled and dove off his horse. I jerked my gun and let Hogarth have it just as he grabbed Tom's and cut loose with it. Maisie hit the ground, too, and commenced clawing sky."

"What did Maisie say?"

"Nothing. Just '*Gracias, amigos.*' "

Johnny's features were sober. "Did Maisie ride back with you?"

Brewster shook his head. "Tom said, 'We might as well take Chris back to the ranch,' and he told Clete, 'You saw it.' Clete said, 'I'm not going to face Connie with you.' He looked right straight at Tom and said, 'One of these days you'll be taking that badge off. Remember that.' "

Johnny considered it, brows knitted. "Treva wasn't told that you shot Hogarth?"

Brewster waved a hand. "Sure, she was told. But Tom was in charge. They'll blame him same as me."

"You're not afraid of them?"

Brewster's lip curled. "I'm not scared of anybody."

"Well, Cade, being a little scared helps sometimes," Johnny said. He got up and rolled the papers back inside his slicker. Soon, then, he headed for the bunkhouse.

CHAPTER XIII

When Johnny McVay reined off the Red River road to put his blazed-face black gelding up among the whitewashed trees of the knoll on which the Casper home sat, it was nearing sunset and the trees were casting long, narrow shade. He noted the ruts of a wagon and the prints of a team coming from the Casper lane to join others and turn north, and Johnny was speculating on it when he stopped his horse at the Casper porch. He saw at once that the house was shut tight. The Caspers, Virgil and Effie and Rebecca, were gone.

Ground-hitching the gelding and untying his saddle strings, Johnny got their blanket and went around the house, looking about carefully. He went behind the smokehouse, doing the same. Everything was as it should be. Virgil had done up his chores before leaving, and he didn't plan to be gone long. The calves were still running with the cows. The dog, locked in the crib, was scratching and howling.

Returning to the house, Johnny found the kitchen door shut but not latched. He went in and helped himself to supper. He put the borrowed blanket and cup on a chair.

A little later, in the saddle again, he went on

down the main road, following the wagon ruts.

Full dark had closed in when he espied lights in a level grove near the creek. The grove was filled with an amazing number of wagons and teams, rigs and saddle horses. Johnny McVay rode in close and tied his gelding to a bush. He walked up to the arbor, which was floored with sawdust and filled with plank benches. Banjo torches flickered on trees roundabout. In the end near the creek, a rustic pulpit had been constructed, and this part was bright with lanterns.

Removing his hat, Johnny McVay looked around, noticing that Billy Phillips had really packed them in. Johnny himself had come here because the young preacher had told him that being obliged wasn't enough—he had to be among Phillips's congregation. Now he was.

Virgil and Effie Casper, wearing their go-to-meeting best, sat in the center front row near the mourners' bench. Rebecca was standing among the choir, all dolled up, pretty as all get-out.

The Reverend Phillips glanced at Rebecca and said something to her that brought a smile. She moved closer and put her curly brown head close to his jaw. They thumbed through her song book together.

Rebecca had forgotten that she had ever planned to marry Sammy Lee Dilts. Billy Phillips wasn't remembering Treva Veblen, now Mrs. Tom Saxon, either.

Another dressed-up clodhopper with a hymnal shouted, "All right, everybody, let's stand! Everybody sing, now!"

As the hymn resounded through the woods, Johnny McVay edged in to an unoccupied place at a bench, but he was afraid really to sing even though he opened his mouth. He figured his voice was too cracked.

When the singing was over, he listened attentively to the young minister expound the Gospel. In his own element here, Billy stuck up mightily for Saint Paul and lambasted Satan up and down and sideways. He hoarsened soon. Finally he began pleading for mourners and the bench quickly filled with kneeling supplicants. Billy moved among them, bending over to hug and comfort each, the deacons helping him.

All in all, Billy had done a pretty good job, brought a fine message, Johnny McVay figured. Still, when the benediction had been spoken, he didn't rush forward as others did to shake Billy's hand. He just stood and looked.

When certain that Billy wasn't going to spend the night with the Caspers, Johnny returned to his horse. . . .

He was seated in the dark of the Caspers' porch when their wagon rolled up the lane.

Virgil stopped to let his womenfolks alight, and Rebecca said apprehensively, "Pa, there's somebody's horse."

"Mine," Johnny said. He fired up a cigarette to illuminate his features.

Virgil said, "We've been to meeting, Johnny. How long you been here?"

"Not long."

"Well, I'll take this team on and peel the harness off."

"You've got the calves to pen, too. Want some help?"

"No. You set still."

Coming onto the porch with her daughter, Mrs. Casper said, "Johnny, why didn't you let that dog out? A body would think that howling would get on your nerves."

"I was afraid he might follow you."

Virgil drove the wagon on to the barnlot. Effie went inside to light a lamp and to open the doors and raise the windows.

Clothes rustling, Rebecca took a seat on the edge of a chair. "You should have been here to attend church with us, Johnny."

"Billy Phillips a pretty good preacher?"

"He's a wonderful preacher."

Mrs. Casper, having lit the lamp in the living room, called, "How did you like that rain, Johnny?"

"That was some rain, a real gully-washer."

Still inspired by the sermon, Rebecca said, "Mother, don't you think Brother Phillips is about the best preacher you ever heard?"

"Well, yes, he's the hellfire-and-brimstone type, no denying that."

"Oh, Mother!"

The dog came upon the porch, sniffing, body and tail both wagging. He stood on his hind legs and almost got his paws on Rebecca's lap.

She slapped him back, saying, "Get down from here, you nasty thing!"

Spot slunk away. He'd trotted through mud and his paws were dirty, but somehow Rebecca's tone hurt Johnny McVay more than it injured the dog.

He snapped his fingers. "Come here, pup," he said, and Spot, rearing up, tried to lick his face.

"He acts like we'd been gone a week," Rebecca said.

"Rebecca," the girl's mother called, "don't you want to get into some cooler things?"

"I guess I'd better." Rebecca got up to go inside. "Are you going to stay a while, Johnny?"

"Not long."

Casper returned from the barnlot. Stamping his feet to remove the mud, he came up and took his favorite chair. "Any word about Sammy Lee?" he asked.

"Not yet. But Uncle Oscar took his trail."

Casper said, "Sheriff Rodin'll get him. What do you reckon will happen then?"

Johnny wouldn't speculate.

The womenfolks came out and sat down, and the talk turned again to affairs at the revival meeting.

Johnny didn't visit as long as he had intended to when he'd left the Hooker ranch. Nevertheless it was at a late hour and the stagecoach wasn't far behind him when he reached the corral in town and turned the gelding loose.

Climbing over the gate, he glanced toward the lights of the Silver Saddle, but went along the street to the hotel, not wanting at this hour to disturb Lucy Smollet.

The stagecoach rolled across the bridge as he reached the Tumbleweed veranda. He waited there until certain Sheriff Rodin wasn't on it; then he went through the lobby and upstairs to the corner room. He hit the hay.

By daylight a hot breeze had lifted. Gazing out a south window, Johnny McVay told himself that two hours of this breeze and sunshine would make this town as dusty as ever. Even now dust was being kicked up by a horse on the main thoroughfare. The rider, he saw, was Clete Maisie.

Johnny ate breakfast in the hotel dining room and found himself sitting across the table from the potbellied marshal. Fenwick passed him a telegram. It was from Oscar Rodin and sent from Fort Sumner, New Mexico.

Marshal Fenwick, his pudgy forefinger following the writing on the yellow sheet, read slowly: "Keep eye on Johnny till I get back. Keep him sober. Picked up Sammy's trail here, also a widow. See you."

"Now what the hell does that mean?" Fenwick said, turning his eyes to Johnny. "That last?"

"Maybe Uncle Oscar won't be so lonely any more. Anyhow, he can't say we didn't warn him if he gets dry-gulched."

Marshal Fenwick guffawed. "He ain't saying nothing—if he gets dry-gulched."

"Is Tom Saxon in the office?"

Fenwick nodded. "He got one of these, too. Sammy Lee Dilts squandered Barlow Clesson's poker money at Fort Sumner. Oscar aims to have hisself appointed deputy U.S. marshal so he can have jurisdiction out of the county."

They finished the meal and went out on to the veranda and Johnny McVay soon headed for the courthouse. Emerging from the building just as Johnny came up the stoop, the tawny-haired Saxon stopped abruptly, his expression guarded.

Johnny said, "How's your wife?"

"She's fine." Saxon cleared the doorway and put his back to the masonry ledge. "Johnny, if you'll listen to reason, you'll have something valuable."

"Yeah. A grave."

Saxon gestured with both hands. "No harm done, is there? We thought you might see it our way after the papers were signed. We need you.

If I could buck the Fiddleback alone, I'd have done it a long time ago, for old Joe."

"Why did you use that badge to stir up trouble?"

"It was already stirred up. We declared ourselves when we picked you up off the range. You'd have died there, and that's what the Fiddleback hoped you'd do. Cade said, 'We took sides with McVay, Tom. We've got to hit them and keep hitting them every way we can.'"

Johnny frowned. "I took the slug that was meant for you—the man who'd moved onto that ranch. Hogarth was your friend until then."

Saxon shook his head. "Not a friend. I was with him a lot. With Barlow, too, for that matter. But I've always been on Joe Hooker's side."

Johnny rubbed the back of his neck. "Do you know how much money Barlow let Joe have?"

"No."

"Do you know if he let him have *any?*"

"Joe had money to throw at the birds for a while. It could have been Barlow's. But if Joe borrowed from him, Joe didn't intend to put the ranch up for collateral. I'm sure of that."

"Well," Johnny said, "we'll talk about it later." He turned back down the courthouse steps.

Clete Maisie trailed him when he left the square, although seeming of no mind to overtake him.

During the next couple of hours, Johnny changed his destination several times to keep from meeting Maisie face to face. He was at the public well, getting a drink, when Maisie decided he'd stalked the Wyoming man long enough. When Johnny squared around, he looked into a pair of emotionless pale gray eyes.

The thin-faced man hooked thumbs in the belt which supported his brace of Charter-oak Colts. "McVay, how long will it take you to wind up your business and get out of the valley?"

"Why should I leave?"

"Because I figure you're a threat to the Fiddleback."

"Did you consider Chris Hogarth a threat?"

"He would have been, with Barlow gone."

"When I get ready to leave," Johnny said, "you'll probably hear about it."

Maisie's eyes became slits. "Sundown," he said. "Ride out by then."

Johnny said, "One of us will," but Maisie ignored him now, and walked off toward the blacksmith shop.

Pushing his hat back, Johnny leaned on the water trough. He had some thinking to do.

He was almost at the swinging doors of the Silver Saddle, when he heard his name spoken by Pablo Cardoza. The Mexican was under a tree on the plaza.

Johnny said, "*Que hay*, Pablo?"

Any attempt at Spanish by a gringo always amused the Mexican, and the dark-skinned hombre showed his white teeth. "Something of importance, Juanito."

A jerkline outfit was rolling along the street, and Johnny crossed the thoroughfare almost under the noses of the lead team.

In a tone that would brook no refusal, Pablo said, "Come with me a little minute," and started off, walking fast. Johnny McVay went with him.

They angled across the square, passing the corner of the courthouse, and continued across the side street to the corrals. A tall board fence separated this corral from that of Wells Fargo & Company. Men and horses were there, but Johnny couldn't see them or hear them when he followed Pablo into the dim, litter-covered interior of the stable on the back of the lot.

Connie Clesson and her pinto pony were there.

Doffing his sombrero and bowing low, Pablo said, "*El sobrino, senorita.*"

"Wait for me," she told him.

With another bow, Pablo backed away, turned and put on his hat.

The stable was sultry but Connie appeared impervious to the heat. She always looked the same when she came to town horseback—dainty boots and spurs, doeskin divided skirt and satin blouse. Framed by the chin strap, her lovely face was enigmatic. Sinking onto the litter near the nose of her pony, she laid her hat aside. Johnny settled down chuck-wagon fashion to face her and put his hat beside hers.

"Clete ordered you out of the valley?"

Johnny nodded. "I guess it was an order."

She grimaced. "I told him not to do that." She kept her gaze lowered and said, "With Barlow and Chris in their graves, Clete has set out to be boss."

"Well," Johnny said, "don't worry about it, Connie. I've been ordered out of places before."

Cheeks stained with color, she looked at him. "I'm not worried about you. You can take care of yourself. I'm thinking of Connie. Pretty soon I won't have a doggoned thing to say about my own ranch." She picked up a straw and chewed on it.

"Clete's always been loyal to the brand."

"That's what you told me. Uncle Oscar said he'd been tolerably friendly with Joe Hooker, too."

"Friendly enough to order Joe away from there," Connie said. She straightened her legs and leaned on a braced palm. "Do you think Treva needs that place? Eric Veblen is rich, and she'll get it all eventually. The only reason she's the least bit interested is because Tom Saxon wants to live there. And we bought it, darn it."

"I believe you. Did you know they're married?"

Connie gave him a long look. "Your feelings hurt?"

"I'll live through it."

Connie smoothed her skirt. "Everyone knew they'd get married sooner or later, when Tom could bring Eric around to it. After Eric made a sieve out of that tinhorn gambler, Tom probably decided Eric would want to keep his nose clean, and took a chance. You can't tell about Eric, though—what he'll do."

Johnny said, "From what I've heard, Eric shouldn't have rushed things."

"That's right. We'd have taken care of Minch, strung him up out there on the plaza."

"Uncle Oscar thinks he'll be bringing Sammy Lee Dilts back soon. He wired Saxon he'd picked up the trail at Fort Sumner."

Connie nodded. "Where he blew in Barlow's money. That clodhopper will get his needings."

"Better let the law handle it."

Connie shrugged. "I know that better than you do. Losing Chris is all the law trouble I can stand." Her eyes were narrow. "It won't be law trouble when Tom Saxon takes off that badge."

Johnny lifted his neckerchief and mopped his brow. "Have you made Clete your foreman?"

Connie nodded. She pulled her legs under her and sat cross-legged, hands relaxed. She said, "If you'll work for us, I'll go hunt him up and take him home. And he won't be hard to get along with, either."

"It's a deal," Johnny said. "Take him home with

you, and I'll wind things up in town here and be out there the day after tomorrow."

Connie held his gaze for a long moment. "You mean it, Johnny?"

He slowly nodded.

She got to her feet and put on her hat. Flipping one rein over the mane of her pinto pony, she took both reins in her left hand, along with a lock of the pinto's mane. She glanced down at Johnny. "Don't make me a promise you won't keep."

"I'll keep it."

He put on his hat and stood erect. He didn't step forward to boost Connie into the saddle. This wasn't Treva, a product of an Eastern school for young females. This was a girl who'd forked a bronc when still wearing diapers. The pony was one she herself had trained. All Johnny McVay did was step aside, for when Connie sprang up, putting weight on the stirrup, the sleepy-looking pony whirled under her, and she was astraddle, riding toward the gate.

Pablo Cardoza reached it before she did, and swung it open for her, removing his sombrero as she rode out. The Mexican deferred to Connie more than to others, Johnny had observed, but he wouldn't defer to a Fiddleback hand.

CHAPTER XIV

When Johnny McVay finally entered the thronged and noisy Silver Saddle Saloon, Eric Veblen was downstairs, playing poker with four ranchers from the upper valley. The fat saloonkeeper saw Johnny first, and called, "Want me, McVay?"

"Yeah, but no hurry."

Veblen put down his cards, pushed back his Windsor chair and got up. He left his chips piled where they were—piled, not stacked. He considered it bad luck to make neat stacks of his chips, and completely disastrous to count them. Lumbering across the sawdust, he didn't exactly walk upstairs with Johnny; he caught hold of a bannister and hauled himself up. He reached the mezzanine puffing.

Besides the massive desk and chairs in Veblen's office, there were a leather sofa, a cabinet, a bookcase with glass doors, shining cuspidors, and framed portraits. Veblen and McVay sat on the sofa, Veblen with his fingers laced and his elbows on spread knees, head tilted.

Johnny said, "Eric, it'll cost you more than a half interest in ten sections of grass and a few fences and log cabins to get Tom Saxon planted."

Veblen straightened up, jowled features

reddening with swift anger. "What are you talking about? I never said I wanted Tom killed."

"Well, the way everyone else tells it, Tom's been afraid to marry Treva on that account."

"Everyone else had better keep their noses out."

"You made that threat."

"I know. But he's married to her now, and it's different." The saloonkeeper relaxed but appeared glum. "I still hate to think of passing on and leaving all I've got to Treva, though. She'll let him run through it."

"Wait a year or so. Treva will probably have a family of her own started, and you can make your will out to your grandchildren."

Veblen was silent, brooding. Finally he said, "I've thought of that. It's one reason I don't want Treva stuck off out there near the mountain. Be no place for young ones, even if they kept a schoolteacher."

Johnny said, "No, it wouldn't." He was hearing piano music. The rise and fall of saloon noises wafted up with sporadic outbursts of talk and laughter.

Veblen said, "I talked Treva into dealing you a half-interest because I was going to help you get the other half. But you shot Joe. Tom and Treva will remember that, and I was hoping we'd have Treva back home in a few months."

"Got room for Tom, too?"

Veblen raised his brows and rubbed his lower

lip. "He's acting like he's going to make her a good husband. It's a big house. I don't see why we couldn't get along."

After a moment, Johnny said, "I had it figured the other way around, Eric. Tom wanted me to show him how to buck the Fiddleback—counted on Uncle Oscar's help, too. When everything was rosy for him and Treva, he'd have tried to buy, or freeze me out. I didn't want that."

"Tom said he thought you was looking at it that way." The fat saloonkeeper appeared perplexed. "There's another side to it. That ranch will keep Tom in the valley. What would he do without it—come and go as he's always done? He might take Treva off and not bring her back. Her and her mother was all the family I had, that I can recollect."

"Eric, you don't want Tom killed, do you? When he takes that badge off, the Fiddleback will probably try to tally him, on account of Hogarth. But you can stop it."

"How?"

"Let Connie have that ranch."

Veblen licked his lips. "She offered twelve thousand dollars for it."

"Tell Treva to take it, and make Connie pay for the stuff Tom's hauled out there, and the horses."

Veblen watched him.

Johnny said, "Connie's got a head on her shoulders. She knows that even if Barlow did pay

Joe for that land, the Fiddleback has got twelve thousand dollars' worth of good out of it since then, counting hay and all."

"I wouldn't want them to get revenge on Tom," Veblen said worriedly.

"Make a deal with Connie, then. And if you do, Eric, I'll guarantee you Tom won't leave the valley. He likes to wear a badge, and Uncle Oscar can keep him wearing one."

Veblen's jowled features brightened. "Sure, he can. Uh-huh. I'd better send for Owen Tyndale and have him get in touch with Connie."

Johnny said, "She may have left town." Standing up, he took the partnership agreement from his pocket and handed it to the saloonkeeper.

Veblen gave him a questioning look.

"Tear it up," Johnny said.

Getting a cuspidor, Veblen sat there with it between his boots and tore the document to bits. He was lost in thought when Johnny started out of the office. Pausing in the doorway, Johnny said, "What time is it?"

"Huh?"

"*Que hora es*? Got a watch on the end of that chain?"

Veblen glanced at his timepiece. "Supper time, straight up and down."

Johnny McVay descended the stairs and left the saloon, repairing to the Smollet home for the evening meal.

When the sun got close to the far-off mountain, he returned to the Silver Saddle.

It still wasn't sundown, but the street in front of the saloon was shaded completely by the plaza trees and the courthouse building when Clete Maisie appeared.

Maisie jerked a swinging door open and held it there with his tall, lean body. His buckskin vest was buttoned tight. His hatbrim was side-rolled and firmly settled, and he'd had a fresh shave.

"Is McVay in here?"

Only a few among the crowd heard him. A man yelled at the piano player, "Hold it, perfessor," and a sudden hush fell. In the quiet the man asked, "How's that, Mr. Maisie?"

"McVay. He's not supposed to be here. Is he?"

Johnny McVay stood at the bar with a line of men on both sides of him. He had already calculated his chances. The slug through the brisket might have slowed his draw. If so, he wouldn't have long to brood about it—not over two or three minutes.

He said, "Clete, I couldn't make it."

Maisie turned to fix his flat gray eyes on the man from Wyoming. He said sarcastically, "What do you want—sympathy or more time?"

"More time."

"You can't have it. I'm going to walk up to the well and back. By then it will be sundown. *Comprende*?"

"Ah, come in and have a drink, Clete, and forget it."

Maisie's lip curled. "Stop begging," he said, and stepped back.

The batwing made a violent swing when Masie released it, and Johnny McVay headed for it. He almost ran. Hand on gun butt, he shoved outside.

The Fiddleback *segundo* was stalking noisily along the boardwalk, going south toward the center of town.

"Clete!"

The shock of Johnny McVay's voice, lethal and taunting, hurt Maisie's eardrums. He whirled about on the soles of his boots. His left hand clawed down, reaching for the notched Colt, just as Johnny figured he would.

Johnny's Remington roared twice. He meant for the first .44 slug to pass to the left of Maisie's waistband. The second one was directed higher and wider. Maisie got the nigh-side Colt from the leather, but one of Johnny's bullets knocked the weapon from Maisie's fingers.

He cried out. He grabbed for his left hand to squeeze the pain from his fingers. The Colt clattered on the board-walk, made a spin and lay near the street-end of a plank.

With powdersmoke coiling before his face, Johnny McVay said, "Try for the other one?"

"No."

Walking closer, leaving the front of the saloon, Johnny said, "Drop your gunbelt."

Maisie released his left hand. He flexed it, as though unable to believe it was still usable. Unbuckling his belt, he lowered it to the sidewalk.

"Step into the street," Johnny said, and when Maisie had gone out far enough, he stopped him. Standing near the man's gunbelt, Johnny observed from an eye corner an aproned bartender and several others in front of the Silver Saddle. He called, "Somebody tell Pablo Cardoza I need him."

The Mexican was among a group on the courthouse stoop, and soon appeared.

Johnny said, "Clete, where's your horse?"

"Livery stable."

"Pablo, go and get Clete's horse."

"But, Juanito, are you sure he rides a horse? Perhaps it is a burro, no?" White teeth flashing, the Mexican cut across the square.

The gunshots had brought people out on the hotel veranda. On this side of the street they had emerged from business places as far up as the Emporium. They began moving closer, one group and then another. Before Pablo returned with the Fiddleback ramrod's claybank, onlookers had converged from all directions. Connie Clesson, however, wasn't among them.

Leading the golden sorrel close, Pablo handed

Maisie the reins, saying, "Be glad he lets you live, *senor*."

Maisie swallowed but said nothing.

Johnny said, "Get his gun yonder and put it in the holster and hang the belt on his saddle."

"*Si*, Juanito."

Maisie licked his dry lips. He started to say, "I'll be back," but recalled a similar instance when he, himself, had killed a man for just such an utterance. "This *isn't* my horse. I'll have to leave it at the Fiddleback."

Johnny cut a glance at the treetops, seeing sunshine there. "We've still got time. Want to take that walk?"

Maisie flexed his left hand. "How can I?"

"Are you going to force me to kill you?"

Fury still glowed in Maisie's eyes but he said, "No. I'll do what you say. There's always a better man."

"Well, you ride home and tell Connie I sent you."

"Do I keep my job?"

Johnny McVay nodded. He gestured at the horse. When Maisie had swung astride the claybank and got the mettlesome animal lined out down the street, Johnny reloaded his .44. He stood there until Maisie's horse had rattled the planks of the bridge and lifted the dust beyond.

Veblen's bartender said, "Drinks on the house, everybody. How about you, McVay?"

"That's my kind of language."

Later, Johnny went in search of Connie Clesson. He didn't find her. According to Deputy Saxon, she and Tyndale had gone up the hill to Veblen's home to see Mrs. Saxon. Finally taking leave of the tawny-haired man, Johnny went back down the stairs and out on the stoop, and met Bedford Polk.

Silk hat canted low on a jaundiced eye, the county attorney caught his arm. "You be more careful, young fellow. I was standing in front of the drugstore, and one of your bullets ricocheted by there, ninety to nothing. You might have killed somebody."

"I'll watch that next time, Mr. Polk."

When Polk had entered the building, Johnny went on down the steps and turned left into the thickening dark under the trees, heading toward the Smollet home. He was still remembering Clete Maisie's eyes, and he walked along chin lowered. His head jerked up suddenly and he retraced his steps, then continued on past the courthouse and cut around the corner toward the corral. A few minutes afterward the hoofs of his gray thundered across the plank bridge, going north.

He held the gray to a steady gait all the way to Little Goose Creek. Passing under the sycamores, he put the horse through the rushing stream and up onto the springy humus of the bosque. He rode on at a fast clip to the fork of the road, and pulled the gray up to blow.

Dismounting, Johnny rolled and lit a cigarette, gazing at the far-off, moonlit mountain. His horse could make it there in time, maybe, but the gray would be jaded, unfit for further riding.

In the woods, back upstream, a screech owl quavered and just after Johnny's hearing picked up the rhythmic pound of hoofbeats. The horse was coming up the Red River road, quite a way off, maybe a little this side of Sammy Lee Dilts's place. By the time Johnny had put out the cigarette with a bootheel, the horsebacker was close.

"What's your hurry?" Johnny called.

The man said, "Whoa," and tightened his reins. He came on at a trot, pulled the horse to a walk, and stopped at a considerable distance. He kept silent.

"Anything wrong, mister?" Johnny asked.

The sodbuster walked his horse closer. "Why, you're the sheriff's nephew, ain't you? Remember me? I'm Saul Delbert. Me and my boy Freddie—"

"I remember you, but I'm still wondering where you're headed and why, this late."

When his thoughts reverted to the purpose of his ride, Saul Delbert's voice thickened with anger.

"Mr. McVay," he said, "I want to show you something."

He dismounted, walked closer and struck a match to illuminate his features.

Johnny emitted a low whistle. "Somebody sure worked you over."

"Virgil Casper."

"Virgil? Why, he seems like a pretty easygoing fellow. You probably hit him."

"Maybe I did, but he made me so blamed mad. That boy I raised, even if the law does want him, is closer to me than to Virgil, ain't he?"

"I'd think so."

"I bought him out, everything but his place. Well, I went over to the Caspers and told them I wanted Sammy Lee's dog. They wouldn't let me have it."

Johnny considered it. The horses stamped and switched, and the gray rolled his bit cricket. Finally Johnny said, "You're headed for town to swear out a warrant against Virgil?"

"Just as fast as I can get there."

"I wouldn't do that, Saul. You're not really hurt, just banged up a little. Go on home and think it over. The dog's not worth losing friends."

"I am going to have that dog, Mr. McVay. Sammy Lee never gave Rebecca that dog. She just claimed it. I'm not going to have her patting Sammy Lee's dog with one hand and holding on to that preacher with the other."

"Doesn't seem right."

Voice glum, Saul Delbert said, "It ain't. They're going to hang Sammy Lee, sure as the world, and I ought to at least have his dog, hadn't I?"

"But when Sammy Lee left, he and Rebecca took the dog. You wait, Saul. Uncle Oscar will bring Sammy Lee back pretty soon, and we'll ask him about it. If he says give you the dog, I'll see that you get it."

Gingerly Saul Delbert touched his bruised face, but said nothing.

"Go on home now, Saul."

"Mr. McVay, I want to do just like you say, but I'll tell you. Virgil ain't very far behind me, and I'm going on to town."

"Well, in that case," Johnny said, "maybe you'd better."

He waited until Delbert was out of hearing distance, and then he swung into his own saddle to ride on toward the moonlit mountain.

CHAPTER XV

Cade Brewster opened his eyes, found the bunkhouse lamplighted, and jerked wide awake. He saw Johnny McVay, and said crankily, "If you're going to sleep here, you can find a bed without waking everybody up, can't you?"

"I'm not going to sleep here," Johnny said. He moved from one man to another and made sure that all were aroused. Brewster watched him with open mouth. He shook Pete Creighton until he got a response, and he nudged Masefield awake. "Roll out, Vern."

"What time is it?"

"After midnight."

Cade Brewster climbed into his pants, thoroughly angered, and sat down again on his bunk.

Johnny said, "Get a move on, Cade. We're going to ride out of here."

"Ride out of here!" Brewster stared at him, brown-stubbled visage set in challenging lines. "Who said so? And where are we going to ride to?"

"Town, I reckon."

Brewster spat on the floor. "Does Tom know you're out here?"

"No."

Brewster's tone eased. "You ain't on a high lonesome, are you, kid?"

"No, I'm not drunk. I'm just trying to keep you from getting killed. The Fiddleback will be here pretty soon."

"You are drunk!"

Masefield said, "Johnny, what makes you think the Fiddleback will raid us?"

"I tangled with Clete. He'll be looking for something to take his spite out on. This place will be it."

Brewster blinked. "Did you beat him to the draw?"

"Well, not the way he wanted me to, but I got my gun out before he did his. Kind of embarrassed him before the whole town."

Cade Brewster glanced from one to another of the men. "Maybe we had better get our clothes on and be ready. We've got long-range rifles now. Up close, our carbines and six-shooters will take care of them."

Johnny said, "Cade, we're not going to fight. We'll ride out and let them have it."

"Like blazes we will! You might be speaking for your part, but I'm talking for Tom Saxon, myself. We fight. He would, by God!"

Flushed with anger again, Brewster put on his hat, stepped into his spurred boots and stood up to stamp them on. He donned shirt, vest and gunbelt.

"Cade," Masefield said, "I believe Johnny knows what he's doing."

Johnny McVay was standing near the doorway. He stepped outside to listen. He heard no hoofbeats, no approaching cavalcade, nor had the Fiddleback already surrounded this place. If so, they would have opened fire on the bunkhouse when the lamps were lit. And the cookshack, too, was lamplighted.

Turning back inside, Johnny said, "You fellows roll your soogans and pack your keepsakes. You won't ever be back."

Brewster said thickly, "Kid, you're plumb loco."

Johnny went on talking to the men. "Don't bother with something you can replace. I'll see that Tom Saxon pays you for it. Shoo-fly's been up for over an hour, and breakfast is ready. You've all got personal mounts. We'll rope them out and stampede the rest."

Brewster bawled, "Wait a minute now! You ain't going to do any such a thing!"

"They're branded, aren't they?"

"Yeah, but if they scatter, we'll have a rough time rounding them up."

"We won't have it to do. Look, Cade. What I'm trying to tell you is that I think Connie Clesson is buying this ranch from Tom's wife, broncs and all."

Brewster laughed. Even Masefield and Creighton smiled. Turning to Masefield, Brewster said,

"How long has the Fiddleback been trying to do that, Vern—for twenty years?"

The grizzled waddy said, "Longer than that."

Johnny McVay was standing near the entrance. Brewster slowly came toward him. The table and chairs and stove were in the north part of the building, with most of the bunks toward the south end. The lamps swung from the rafters. Squaring around with his back to Masefield's bunk, Brewster said, "Kid, when Tom's wife gave you that half-interest, she didn't aim for you—" Brewster broke off and watched Johnny without comprehension.

Johnny was slowly shaking his head. "That partnership deal didn't go through."

Brewster's doubt and indecision vanished. He grinned with savage triumph. "Why are you out here giving orders, then?"

"Because I think I'm doing right."

"Because you're the sheriff's nephew?" Brewster cut a look at Creighton. "I savvy the deal now, Pete. The kid tried to grab a half-interest in this ranch and couldn't get it. Now he's lollygagging around Connie Clesson. If he can get us to ride out, the Fiddleback will have this place."

Johnny said, "Cade, you're awful bullheaded."

Brewster chewed his lip. Jerking a thumb toward the door he said, "Kid, you get gone. Right now. You ain't welcome."

Johnny turned away from him and said, "You rannihans have all got pay coming. Listen to me and you'll get it, no matter what happens. And jobs, too, if you want jobs. I guarantee it."

"Jobs where?" Masefield asked.

"Somewhere. If nowhere else, up in Wyoming on the Crescent Lazy Two."

"You blasted traitor!" Cade bawled.

"You're wrong. It's just that I know a lost cause when I see one. No cows will ever graze this range except Fiddleback critters, unless Fiddleback says so."

Johnny was standing before Brewster, looking straight at him, and Brewster's fist came up fast and exploded against Johnny's jaw.

Johnny staggered backward. Colliding with the log wall near the door, he tried to stay on his feet, but his knees buckled. When they hit the floor, his brow slammed down. Presently he put a hand against the wall and felt his way erect. He shook his head. The fuzziness cleared, and he straightened his hat.

Glaring, Brewster still had his fists knotted.

"Taking advantage of me, Cade."

"I'll do more than that if you don't fork your bronc and get the hell out of here!"

"Can't. I rode him to a frazzle and turned him loose. Figured to rope one out of your corral."

The grizzled Masefield moved up beside them and looked from one to the other. He said to

Johnny, "You haven't got over Hogarth's slug yet."

"I haven't got over Cade's nursing me, either."

"Cade," Masefield said, "go choose you a grizzly bear or a longhorned bull. The kid here can't rough and tumble yet, but you sure would be loco to tackle him with a six-shooter."

With Masefield's eyes leveled on him, Brewster took water. He said, "Aw, I didn't aim to hit him that hard."

Rubbing a fading temple, Masefield moved among the men, appraising them. "If we take sides, I'm on Johnny's," he said.

One of the others said, "We'll all take the same side, whichever it is."

"Cade," Masefield said, "you'd better calm down. Johnny could have tangled with you once before, but he didn't. It was over twenty of those broncs down yonder, as you well remember. He gave you a hundred dollars just to pacify you."

Cutting a quick glance around, Brewster said, "You fellers do what you want to. I'm going to get the rest of my sleep."

They watched him shuck off his clothes again.

"You'll be here by yourself."

"And I'll be here when you fellers come crawling back with your tails between your legs, wishing you had jobs," Brewster said. He crawled into his bunk.

Johnny McVay walked out into the moonlight.

Masefield, the last to leave the bunkhouse, said, "Cade, do you want me to blow out the lamps?"

Brewster's tone was sarcastic. "No. Leave them burning for the Fiddleback to shoot out."

Shaking his head, Masefield shouldered his bedroll, picked up his carbine and left. He followed the others to the saddle shed. Johnny McVay had heaved his onto the fence. Only Pete Creighton entered the moonlit corral to work his way among the mustangs. Knowing them, he dabbed a loop over each man's mount. He caught two for Johnny. Saddles cinched on, bedrolls tied, they forked their broncs and rode into the corral to haze the remuda out. Some of the geldings, tails streaming high, thundered south among the buildings. When the last bronc had singlefooted north onto the meadow, Johnny McVay asked, "All the barns and stalls empty, too, Pete?"

"They're all empty, Johnny."

"Let's shut the doors and close the gates, then."

Soon, when the men had taken their places at the table, Shoo-fly Flynn served hot sourdough biscuits, bacon, sorghum and coffee. Johnny downed a cup of the scalding coffee and left the others eating. He went out to help Shoo-fly pack his thirty years' gather. They used the back door. Johnny stood there as the sorrel-topped old *cocinero* adjusted the saddlebags and cantle pack to suit himself.

Shoo-fly said, "Why didn't you explain it to them?"

"I got knocked down for explaining as much as I did."

"Cade ought to see it. If Connie did buy this place and Maisie raids it, you'll have Maisie's job."

"Wouldn't matter. Cade would still be right where he is."

Johnny moved off a little way to listen. When he was beside the cook again, Shoo-fly said, "If us fellows meet that stagecoach and I decide to board it, I'll send this horse on to town for you to sell. What do you want me to tell your ma?"

Johnny thought about it. "You might tell her I've got her grandchildren's ma already picked out. All I have to do is win her."

"Making any headway with her?"

"Some."

Slapping his horse on the hip, Shoo-fly said, "Let's see if those fellows are through eating." They went back inside.

The others had left the table and were standing in front of the building near their broncs. Shoo-fly Flynn groaned at the mess he was leaving in the cookshack.

Continuing on through the building, Johnny said, "Mount up," and swung into his own saddle. He led the cavalcade back past the corrals and onto the meadow. High on the moonlit rim of the barranca a white stallion appeared, rearing and pawing and trumpeting; then he was gone.

Jogging along near Johnny, Masefield said, "They could hit us from this direction."

"If they do, Vern, we'll fight for all we're worth. We're trying to ride out peaceable."

Jogging into the timber that fringed Big Goose Creek, Johnny drew rein. The others came to a stop among the trees around him, some of the horses fidgeting.

"We could have ridden up the draw, of course, but I was afraid we'd run head-on into them. Let's follow the creek for a little way and then climb the ridge. We'll come back to that stand of blackjacks yonder on the bluff, and see what happens."

Nobody spoke.

"Or, if you want to," Johnny continued, "you can head for town, get rooms at the Hotel Tumbleweed, and I'll foot the bill till we get things straightened out."

Masefield said, "Take our meals there, too?"

"Of course."

All were silent. Finally Masefield spoke. "Let's ride up on the ridge, like you said."

They followed the creek and presently ascended the slope but not quite to the summit of the ridge, not wanting to be skylined in the moonlight. When even with the blackjacks, they dismounted on the steep incline and led their horses up. They tied them to the stunted trees and moved on to the rim of the bluff. Hunkering down, they looked and listened. Coyotes yapped. The strange noises of night birds came to them. They heard hoofbeats, but having stampeded their own remuda, they couldn't be sure. The hoofbeats grew remote, died away. An hour passed, incredibly slow.

The lights in the cookshack and bunkhouse down there still gleamed. The darkened ranch house and outbuildings cast darker shadows in the moonlight that made a pattern of angles.

Shoo-fly Flynn said, "Johnny, it looks like—"

"We're getting paid for our time," Masefield broke in.

Once more they heard hoofbeats. The drumming grew in volume until it was a furious rataplan. The sound was approaching from the south, along the Fiddleback trail. The trail itself, in the dark shadow of the barranca, couldn't be seen.

"Sounds like the whole Fiddleback outfit," Masefield said.

Nobody else spoke. A couple of the men changed positions in order to get a better view, and they saw a strung-out cavalcade cut away from the shadow of the cliff to head across the alluvial fan toward the ranch buildings.

Gunfire broke out when they were among the buildings, the reports of their weapons reverberating loud in the morning air. They heard shouting. They saw Cade Brewster's underwear-clad silhouette in the bunkhouse doorway.

"Hold your fire!" he bawled. "I'm the only one here!"

Clete Maisie's voice rang out. "Don't shoot him, boys."

"Chris Hogarth wouldn't say that," another yelled, and a fusillade of shots followed his words.

Grabbing his mid-section, Brewster began coughing. He lurched from side to side and turned around. He pitched onto his face on the floor of the bunkhouse.

The loud talking and the gunfire ceased. The horses no longer tore around full tilt, but men rode here and there in the moonlight. The lamplight still shone, and horses were tethered at the cookshack. One man, speaking in a tone that carried to the bluff, asked, "Got some left?" The reply, if any, was pitched low.

"Look; they've set the barn on fire," Masefield exclaimed.

"They're setting everything on fire."

Soon tongues of flame were licking up around the bunkhouse logs.

"Did they drag Brewster out?" Shoo-fly asked.

"No." After a moment, Johnny McVay said, "I've seen enough." All were ready to ride.

Later, drawing rein on the same ridge three

miles east of the stand of blackjacks, Johnny and the others glanced west again, at the red glow flickering on the flanks of the mountain. It sickened Johnny a little. It seemed he could still hear the popping and cracking of the flames, still smell the acrid fumes of the holocaust. It would have made a good ranch, he reflected. It really would have.

"You rannihans cut toward the main road and Little Goose Creek. Shoo-fly, you may meet the stage along there somewhere. I'll see you. I've blazed a trail straight through here to Virgil Casper's place, and I'm going there."

"Be back in a day or so?" Masefield asked.

"Hope to."

"Any orders?"

"Nothing, except stay out of trouble, Vern," Johnny told him. And Masefield vowed that they would.

CHAPTER XVI

Lucy Smollet was letting her baby nurse, and the chair in which she gently rocked squeaked rhythmically. Lamplight spilled through the living room doorway behind her and to her left, dimly illuminating the porch steps and part of the yard. Through the morning-glory vines in front of her glimmered light from the Emporium and from the busy, noisy wagon yard. Lifted by horsebackers headed toward the upper valley, flour-fine dust filled the air, and Lucy could smell it and taste it. Along with the thud of hoofbeats and occasional outbursts of talk over at the Emporium, she heard, between chair squeaks, the myriad small evening noises which comprised her part of the town.

The rattle of the bucket down at the public well reached her, and she recalled what Wade had said when she'd wanted to know why the town didn't install a pump. As far as it was to water, a man could draw three buckets while pumping one, it took so long to get a pump to flow. Of course, Wade might have told her that because he suspected she was getting ready to ask for a pump in their back yard.

The baby had stopped nursing and she burped him and now he lay relaxed in Lucy's arms. His eyes were closed. Lucy stopped rocking and sat there a moment, and then, carefully, she started to rise, to put the child to bed. The baby stiffened. He wriggled to sit up.

"Oh, fiddlesticks, Mike!"

Johnny McVay, arriving at her gate just then, said, "Here now, Lucy. You quit fussing at him."

"Oh, he won't go to sleep." Getting up, Lucy brought the child into the lamplight, asking, "Didn't Oscar come with you?"

"He'll be on in a little bit." Johnny had come into the periphery of the lamplight himself now, and Lucy saw not only him, but the brown-and-white mongrel beside him.

"Why, Johnny, where did you get him?"

"Down Little Goose Creek, it's Sammy Lee Dilts's dog."

After a silence, Lucy said, "I wonder what they'll do to that man."

"He aims to plead guilty. It'll be up to the judge. Sammy Lee may get the penitentiary, but I doubt it. Probably be hanged."

"Hanging him won't bring Wade back."

"But it may keep some other lawman's wife from becoming a widow. My new Aunt Caroline, maybe. She's a real good woman, and I think she'll work out fine for Uncle Oscar." Johnny gathered in more of the chain and said, "Lucy, Spot isn't used to this collar and chain. Be all right if I lock him in your barn till morning?"

"Of course you can. Poor thing, he acts like a whipped dog, sure enough. He hasn't got the mange or anything, has he?"

"Right now he's healthier and cleaner than I am."

Lucy said, "Guess you're both hungry?"

"Yes, ma'am. But don't build up a fire and get the house hot."

Taking the mongrel around the house and into the barnlot, Johnny lifted him into the crib where Wade Smollet had kept corn for the county horse he'd stabled here at night for emergencies. When the chain was unsnapped, the dog licked Johnny's hand and thumped the floor with his tail. Johnny brought a pan of water and fed Spot the table scraps Lucy brought out.

Afterward, Johnny divested himself of dust and sweat, and sat down at the kitchen table.

Having already eaten, Lucy went into the living room, where she had spread a pallet for the baby. After a time she heard Johnny leave the table. Knowing what he would do if not stopped, she called, "Now, don't you bother with those dishes."

"I believe I will let you do them tonight, Lucy. I'm plumb tuckered out."

Johnny was in the front yard, smoking a cigarette. Lucy was sitting in the shadows of the porch, and Mike was on the pallet just inside the doorway, when Sheriff Rodin's gaunt body was limned in the lights of the Emporium. Letting himself into the yard, Rodin brushed his chin whiskers and glanced around.

"Johnny, what did you do with the dog?"

"Put him in the barn."

Ascending the porch steps, Rodin doffed his high-peaked hat. He said, "Evenin', Lucy," and continued on into the living room. He tossed his hat onto the rug near the propped-back door, and stood there looking down at the child.

Firmly planted on his diaper-clad bottom, fat legs thrust out before him, Mike was trying to reach a calico-covered spotted horse without having to move.

Hunkering down, the sheriff pushed the toy closer. Mike ignored it. Rodin picked it up and put it in the child's fist. Mike hurled it aside. He was watching the sheriff expectantly. Rodin held out his hands. The child lifted his arms.

"You little son-of-a-gun," Rodin said, grinning, and picked Mike up. Holding one spread hand under the child's diaper and the other against Mike's bare belly, Rodin lifted him until his head bumped the ceiling.

From the chair behind the vines, Lucy called, "Don't you drop him, Oscar." She could tell by the child's utterances exactly what Rodin was doing. Presently the sheriff brought the young one out on the porch.

Reaching for him, Lucy said, "Yes, you can

always pick him up, but you can't put him down. Go to sleep now, Mike."

The child always yowled when the sheriff sought to leave.

Lucy crooned to the baby and rocked the squeaking chair. Rodin sat down nearby. Johnny McVay took a seat on the edge of the porch, back to a post, one boot planted on the porch, the other on the second step.

Sheriff Rodin, resuming a conversation begun two hours ago in his office, said, "Johnny, you and me and Tom will cut the cards. Low man shoots him."

"You and Tom can. I won't shoot him."

Lucy stopped rocking. "Shoot who?"

"That dog," Rodin said.

Voice thin, Lucy said, "Why do you have to shoot him? Johnny said he was healthy."

"We have to make Tom Saxon's word good. Some Goose Creek nesters got into a squabble, both wanting the dog. Tom told them to wait till I brought Sammy Lee back, and he would do whatever Sammy Lee said to do. Sammy Lee didn't want either one of them to have it."

"And he said shoot it?"

"Uh-huh," Johnny said.

After a silence, Lucy said, "Well, I won't let you do it, Johnny. You hear me?"

Sheriff Rodin showed quick interest. "We'd hate to. You need a dog around here, Lucy. That boy is getting bigger every day, and I wouldn't think of—" The sheriff coughed.

Johnny broke in, "Nobody ought to try to raise a boy without a dog. Ain't I right, Uncle Oscar?"

"If I had a boy that size, I'd want him to own a dog. But how'll you talk Tom out of it, and keep Casper and Delbert off his neck?"

"We'll ask Sammy Lee. We didn't mention Wade's young one."

Lucy thought about it. She said, "I'd have to let that dog run loose, and he'd be in and out of the house all the time. I'd have to keep an eye on Mike twenty-four hours a day." She started rocking again.

"Mike asleep?" Johnny asked.

"His eyes are as big as saucers."

"Uh-huh. I'll get that dog and let's see how he acts around younguns."

Johnny didn't snap the chain on Spot. The dog followed him out of the barnlot and sat down and waited for him to latch the gate. He kept close to Johnny as they went around the house. He came up on the porch but stopped there, one paw lifted.

"Come on now," Johnny coaxed. He caught hold of the collar and dragged Spot inside.

The baby was on the pallet. Sheriff Rodin and Lucy sat on the couch.

Spot didn't growl, but he struggled to get away. Once he nipped at Johnny's hand. On his knees,

Johnny got a shoulder behind Spot and a grip on Spot's collar and foreleg. He pushed Spot close. Mike raised a hand. Spot flinched. Johnny tripped him and made him lie on his side.

Scooting forward, Mike slapped first one fist and then the other on Spot's ribs. Johnny loosened his hold. Spot crept off the pallet. He stood near the dining-room partition, licking his chops and looking from one to another.

Mike crawled off the pallet. When the baby got close, Spot sidled past him and Johnny and headed for the front door. He didn't go out. He looked back at Johnny and sat down. Mike began crawling toward him. Suddenly the child bowed his back and pushed to his hands and feet. He stood erect and toddled forward, elbows swinging.

"He's walking!" Lucy cried. She sprang up and grabbed Mike, eyes shining.

Johnny said, "Ain't no need of locking that dog in the barn, I guess."

"He's a good dog," Lucy said. "He won't bother."

Johnny put his gaze on the door. He said to Spot, "You can go out now," and the dog darted outside. Once during the night, Spot's barking aroused Johnny, but it was just someone passing along the street with a dog that tried to fight Spot through the fence. If the fence hadn't been there, though, the dog wouldn't have wanted to fight.

The owner whistled his dog away, and Johnny heard no more.

Saying it was too hot to sleep two in a bed, Sheriff Rodin had repaired to the hotel. . . .

He and Tom Saxon were both in the office around nine o'clock when Johnny McVay got there. Saxon had taken Sammy Lee Dilts's breakfast to him before the sheriff's arrival. Not knowing, therefore, that Lucy Smollet wanted the dog, the deputy hadn't mentioned it.

Seeing Johnny, Sheriff Rodin came out of his chair, saying, "Well, let's go back and find out if we have to shoot the pooch."

The tawny-haired Saxon led the way to the cell block. Here the windows were small, and the sunlight at this hour didn't filter through. The cell in which Dilts had been locked was dark and gloomy.

Catching hold of a bar higher than his head, Deputy Saxon stood there hipshot. "Sammy Lee," he said, "if we could afford to give you a gun, we'd bring Spot up here and let you shoot him. I'd rather put a slug between your eyes than Spot's."

Hair tousled, the big-boned young killer was sitting on his bunk. He glanced sourly at Rodin and McVay and said to Saxon, "If I hadn't doubled back to Fort Sumner, I'd have come and got Spot before long."

Rodin said, "Why do you want him to die?"

Sammy Lee stood up, features worried. "Well, I won't be around to see that he gets taken care of. I wouldn't trust him with Saul or Virgil, either."

Rodin said, "I'll find him a good home."

Sammy Lee glared at him. "Shoot him, I told you."

Saxon let his arm fall. He straightened his body and tipped his hat lower. He said, "Deputy Smollet's widow wants Spot. She's got—"

Sammy Lee's features went savage. "Yeah. Got a baby boy, and he ain't got no father. Rodin reminded me of that a hundred times."

Saxon glanced at the sheriff. "If he wants that dog shot, I can sure shoot it. Let's go."

"Oh, go ahead and let her have him," Sammy Lee blurted. "What's a little old no-good dog?" He turned away and threw himself onto his bunk, stretching out on his back.

The three men went up the corridor.

Turning into the office, Sheriff Rodin headed for his desk. Saxon walked to a front window and looked down at the plaza. Johnny McVay leaned against the ledge of the south windows.

"Treva coming for you, Tom?" the sheriff asked.

"Said she would."

Johnny said, "Were those fellows fair about the stuff they lost in the fire?"

"I don't know," Saxon said. "I settled with them at their own figures."

"They all leave town?"

"All of my trail hands. Masefield and Creighton are waiting to see you."

Johnny reached for the makings. "I'll probably put them to work."

Saxon said, "Hope it's not on the Fiddleback, but even if it is, Treva and I won't have any say-so about that north range now. She deeded it to Connie."

Sheriff Rodin said, "Me, I'd of buffaloed Brewster and packed him away from there, hanging over his saddle."

"Me, I didn't feel big enough to," Johnny said. He looked at Saxon. "Going to keep wearing that badge?"

"I'm going to run against Oscar next election."

Rodin said, "If he beats me, I'll be deputy, and if I'm re-elected, we'll go on like it is."

"Seems tricky to me," Johnny said.

"Politics," Rodin told him.

Straightening, Johnny turned to the open window, looking at the horseshoe game in progress below. Fenwick and Tyndale and Bedford Polk were among the spectators. Through the trees, Johnny could see the main intersection and the sixteen-mule jerkline outfit that had lined out down the dusty thoroughfare. The big Murphy wagon and back-action would be fording Little Goose Creek before long. For such a freighting outfit to travel that road safely seemed impossible, just looking at the wagons, but they had been doing it for years.

"Here comes the Fiddleback," Saxon said, and remotely Johnny heard the rattling bridge timbers.

When he had crossed to the window beside Saxon, both men saw a team of sorrels and a sparkling buggy arriving on the plaza below. It was Treva.

Johnny said, "Can she handle a team?"

"She can handle those sorrels," Saxon said. He turned to the sheriff. "Want me back about dark, Oscar?"

"Uh-huh. Along about dark."

"Maybe," Saxon said, "I can get gone before Connie sees me."

"She won't blame you," Johnny told him. "There are loyal men in her outfit. She'll know Maisie did it."

He and Saxon left the office together.

CHAPTER XVII

Dust fogged when the Fiddleback *corrida* hit the end of the main street, where they checked their racing horses. They reined toward the Hotel Tumbleweed and pulled up in a group in front of the veranda. Wearing the familiar blue blouse and divided doeskin skirt, Connie Clesson lifted a leg over the saddle and hit the ground. McVickers took the reins of her pinto pony. Undoubtedly worn out from the early rising and the long ride, Connie nevertheless ran up the veranda steps.

Masefield and Creighton leaned against the railing. Connie paused to speak to these men before entering the lobby. The Fiddleback outfit rode on to the center of town and dismounted at the public water trough.

Only men were on the hotel veranda when Johnny McVay got there. He said to Masefield and Creighton, "You rannihans getting tired of waiting?"

"No," Masefield said. "Like I told Pete the other night, Johnny, I think you know what you're doing."

Creighton said, "Johnny, me and Vern ain't gunslingers. Don't hire us out for that. We're just cowhands and maybe not very good ones."

"Pete, you've got cow-savvy and horse-savvy,

too. And patience," Johnny said. He rolled and lit a cigarette and took a chair in the row against the wall. He asked then, "What did Connie say, besides howdy?"

Masefield said, "She told us she'd bought the mustangs we stampeded and asked us if we wanted to help round them up. I told her to see you, and she asked where you were."

"I saw you pointing at me."

"Yeah. And she said she'd go wash her face and talk with you."

"She looked sort of mad," Creighton added.

It was fifteen minutes before Connie reappeared. Her tanned countenance had a freshly scrubbed look, and her light blond hair was still damp at the temples. Her dark eyes, however, were obscure.

Johnny's chair was near the door. Emerging from the lobby, Connie put a hand on his shoulder. "Come on. Let's go up to the restaurant. I've got to have some coffee."

"You ought to go to bed and sleep a while," Johnny said, but he got up to follow her down the steps.

They crossed the side street and passed under the plaza trees, both silent. When even with the courthouse, they reached the tree which cast the deepest shade.

"Let's rest here a minute. I want to talk to you,"

Connie said. She sank down upon the grass and took off her hat, fanning with it for a moment. "You heard about my bad luck, didn't you? I bought Treva's ranch and when I got home, the boys told me they'd raided that place. Burned most of the buildings."

"Tell you about shooting Brewster and burning him, too?"

They had told her, and Connie gave him an answer with her lips closed.

Having stabled their horses, the Fiddleback men were coming past the blacksmith shop. Johnny watched them turn the bank corner, going toward the restaurant, too.

Connie put her hat back on. She pulled her crossed legs under her and watched Johnny McVay's profile. He had his boots crossed, legs stretched out, an elbow braced on the grass.

She said, "Clete wouldn't go home with me, and he said you couldn't work for us."

Johnny looked at her.

"How am I going to fire him?" she wanted to know.

"Pay him what you owe him and tell him to light a shuck."

"But he won't do it."

"Want me to kill him?"

Dainty features contorting, Connie said, "I just want to fire him and have him stay fired."

"What did he say?"

"Well, I told him he was through for making that raid. He said it wasn't right because he had no way of knowing about my deal with Treva. I'd told him once before we had ought to do that, if—if anyone moved onto the Hooker place."

"Your crew sided with him," Johnny said.

The girl nodded. She said, "You're faster with a gun than he is, aren't you?"

"Yes. But if Clete's as loyal to your brand as you say he is, I don't see any need for letting him go. Listen to him once in a while. Maybe you won't have so much trouble."

"Don't you want that job yourself?"

Johnny shook his head. "I'm leaving."

"You don't like it here?"

"Oh, I like it all right, but I belong up in Wyoming. I've got a lot of things to do up there."

She moistened her lips. Her eyes showed strain. "When are you leaving?"

"*Manana.*"

"It never comes."

"This one will."

"Gee, I didn't know you were leaving that soon." She averted her face for a moment and said, "I'd better tell you good-by now."

"Yes, or *hasta la vista.*"

"No, Johnny. I don't think we'll ever meet again."

A few moments later, Johnny McVay stood watching Connie walk on toward the restaurant.

When she rounded the corner of the bank building, he turned and set out in the opposite direction. His homely face was one big grin. Thinking back, he wanted to shake hands with himself.

That Connie! She was cute as a little red wagon, and, if she would take Clete Maisie's advice once in a while, she'd have one of the best spreads in north Texas. And thinking of the firm set of her jaw and her up-turned nose, Johnny knew that whoever married her would have to be Mister Connie Clesson, right down the line. Johnny McVay shook his head and walked faster.

And Treva. Why, Johnny must have been as loco as a sheepherder to think that she could have made a wife for a young rancher who'd have to start from scratch up in Wyoming. Johnny grinned a bit ruefully. But she could sure play poker like all get-out! And as a town girl, the wife of a politicking deputy who would probably some day end up in the state legislature in Austin, she'd do just fine. Set her down in the middle of a few square miles of Wyoming range, riding herd on a one-room log cabin or helping snake a balky steer out of a bog, and she'd be completely lost. Rebecca Casper maybe could handle a job like that. Johnny rubbed the side of his face, remembering the swinging coffee pot and recalling, too, her anger when Spot came up on the porch with muddy paws. But Rebecca could sure help corral a congregation for the Reverend Billy Phillips and boss a Ladies' Aid tea party without any sweat at all. . . .

At the driveway beside the morning-glory covered porch he turned in. From the kitchen came the comfortable early evening sounds of Lucy rattling pots and pans in the kitchen and he heard her singing to Mike. He went up the steps to the kitchen door and said, "Hi, Lucy."

She looked up, brushing back a wisp of red hair from her eyes. "Hello, Johnny. Come inside."

From her arm, Mike began to make happy noises, and when she set him down, he started to toddle over to Johnny, then fell on his face and, still laughing, got up again. Johnny stooped, lifted him up and tossed him toward the ceiling, then caught him and set him down.

"Wow!" Johnny grinned. "You're either getting heavier or I'm getting weaker." He stopped, his face hot, a lot of words choking in his throat. "Uh—Lucy—" he managed.

"Yes, Johnny?"

"Lucy, I—I—Well, I've come to say good-by. I'm going back tomorrow. Back to Wyoming, that is."

"I'm sorry to hear you say that, Johnny."

"What I mean is, Lucy, that I aim to ride back to Grief Hill before long. I'd like to see you, if you're still here. That is, I—"

"Why, Johnny McVay! Where on earth else would I be but right here?"

At the strange huskiness in her voice, Johnny looked at her. She was leaning back against a table, her knuckles white on its edge. He looked into her eyes and saw a single tear slowly form and zigzag down her cheek. She did not utter a sound. And that did it.

Without thinking, he felt his arms go about her, felt her solid softness melt against him and he leaned down, his lips close to her ear, one hand smoothing her forehead. And then the words tumbled out, words that he had wondered if he could ever find the courage to say to this girl, so soon after Wade had died.

He told her that he had taken an option on a few parcels of good land next to the Crescent Lazy 2, and had enough money to buy a small herd of whitefaces, as a starter. He had arranged for Masefield and Creighton to help him build a cabin, which could be added on to as time went by. She wouldn't be all alone, because his ma and step-pa would drop in, and most of the Crescent hands he had known since he'd been as young as Mike, here. And he'd do his best to make her and Mike happy—

She held him off, her hands still clutching his shoulders. "Why, Johnny," she said, laughing and crying at the same time, "thanks so much for the invitation. But isn't it—"

"I know it's awful soon, Lucy. I—I mean, after what you've been through, and all. So just take your time, honey, and—"

"It isn't all that," she said gravely. "But isn't it customary, if you want Mike and me that much, to say something about getting married?"

As Johnny had said, he had a lot of things to do up in Wyoming, and it was almost a year later before he felt he was settled enough to call for Lucy and Mike. The original one-room log cabin he had planned had, in the process of building, miraculously grown to a rambling four-room ranch house—with still room for additions as needed.

His ma had helped furnish it, saying, " 'Course, I know Lucy'll probably have her own ideas about how she wants things, but anyhow, this will do to start her off," and Ian MacVarish had stood by, nodding approval and smoking his pipe. "I've got four sections of good graze, lad, that I'll lease to ye anytime you say."

The boss of the Crossed JL slung his warsack in the rear of the new spring buggy, picked up the reins and the matched team of bays started south, sunlight sparkling on the red wheels.

His ma waved to him, wiping her eye with the corner of her gingham apron, while bearded Ian sat his horse, removing his pipe long enough to shout: "Take good care of the wee bairn, noo,

Johnny. He'll make a fine decoy for a lot more!"

Johnny McVay didn't hear his step-pa, but he turned and waved through the billowing dust cloud behind him.

Texas redhead, here we come!

Center Point Large Print
600 Brooks Road / PO Box 1
Thorndike, ME 04986-0001 USA

(207) 568-3717

US & Canada:
1 800 929-9108
www.centerpointlargeprint.com